ANNIE LEE

* * * * * * * *

Keeping Grace Alive

* * * * * * * *

First Novel in the Pocono Mountains Series

CHANCES 'R' PUBLICATIONS

PRINTING HISTORY
Tobias Book edition / February 2011
CHANCES 🐴 PUBLICATIONS February 2012

Published by CHANCES 🐴 PUBLICATIONS, Ocala, Florida.
www.chancesrpublications.wordpress.com

Visit our website at **AnnieLeeNovelist.com**.
Join us on Facebook at the **Annie Lee Fan Page**.
Join the Keeping Grace Alive book page on Facebook to keep in touch with other book lovers.

Cover design by CHANCES 🐴 PUBLICATIONS

A Special Thanks

First and foremost, I have to thank the love of my life: my son, Matthew. He gives me a determination and a drive to become the best I can be at whatever endeavor I am pursuing.

To Toby, the most trustworthy and loved Yellow Lab in the world, this book would not be complete without your slobber on the pages of every edited draft, or your one-hundred-and-thirty pound body lying across my lap as I write.

To Pediatric Associates of Ocala, you not only take the most amazing care of my son, but you also have been the first to allow me to advertise my book and help me advertise my work.

A special thanks to Lori McCormick, Danielle Cayea Johnson, Becky Roach, Darlene Gray, and Carol Mellon for reading my book before publication and providing amazing feedback.

And to my zoo. To Daisy, for lying next to me in bed on the late nights when one of my novel plots is in my head and I just have to get it down. To Stormy for waking me up the next morning after those late nights. To Toby because I just love you more than words can say. To Elle, for always being excited to see me. To the fish & turtle, for not dying for Matthew's sake. To the toads in the yard that keep Matthew busy so mommy can write. To the Guinea Pigs, which provide every animal member of our family with constant entertainment.

And finally, to all my fans! I hope you enjoy my books and keep coming back to read more of them. I love hearing from you so please write to me on my website or send an e-mail. Enjoy my novel!

~Annie

"Love is patient, love is kind. It does not envy, it does not boast, it is not proud. It is not rude, it is not self-seeking. It is not easily angered, it keeps no record of wrongs. Love does not delight in evil but rejoices in truth. It always protects, always trusts, always hopes, always perseveres.

And now these three things remain: faith, hope and love. But the greatest of these is love."

1 Corinthians 13:4-7, 13

To my son. Who has, without failure, been my life, my light, my love. I would never have made it without you. I owe my life to you.

* * * * * * * *

Keeping Grace Alive

* * * * * * * *

First Novel in the Pocono Mountains Series

Chapter One

Jessie sat around the table with his four brothers. By blood, they were strangers. By years of camaraderie, they were brothers.

"This isn't like our past attempts to keep Gracie safe." The seriousness in Jessie's voice spoke of the danger she was in. "If we don't safely get her out of here tomorrow night, Phillip will get her. Rudy told me himself tonight."

Rudy Talbot, head of one of the largest organized crime rings in the United States, was running for State Attorney General in the upcoming March elections. He had his sights set on a government position for years. It would solidify his power and give him an upper hand in the justice system. Should he win, he would be an unstoppable force of governing power and corruption.

Two things were keeping this greedy, power-dominated man from his title: political support and his rebellious socialite stepdaughter Grace Talbot, or "Gracie" as everyone called her.

Finding political support was easy enough. Current lame duck Senator Dennis Proctor came to Rudy with an offer he couldn't refuse. In exchange for political support, Dennis' son was to marry Gracie. Since Phillip Proctor was running for his father's seat, he needed a wife and an image someone like Gracie could provide. She came from money, her stepfather would most likely win State

Attorney General, and she appealed to the public with her beauty and all-American charm. Quite simply, Phillip and Rudy could not win the election without her.

"What are they going to do to her?" Clyde asked.

"Kill her."

Rudy had enough of Gracie and wanted to be done dealing with her. Gracie cost Rudy the past two elections. But with Phillip in the running now, he couldn't give up the alliance and the support the Proctors offered him. Gracie had to cooperate. They would make her.

"Stick to the plan. Me and Clyde will enter the front doors. Clyde will watch the front door while I head around to the back of the counter. Bubba, you and Peter will enter in the back. Peter will help me force the girls into the back room where Rudy can't see what we're doing. This is the most important part. We have to get them out of sight from the front windows. You know Rudy will be watching from the parking lot across the street. Clyde, you'll stay in the front room for crowd control. Go to the cash register first, break the lock and take what's in the safe. We need to make this look like a robbery. Bubba, help me tie up the girls, except for Gracie. I'll get her. No one is to touch her, understood?"

Everyone nodded in agreement.

"As soon as all the workers are tied up, I'm going to shoot a couple of rounds in the back. Clyde, that's your cue to get to the back of the store as quickly as you can. Derek will have the van pulled up to the back of the shop, so we should be able to climb right in without anyone seeing us. The goal is to get Gracie out of Orlando, and keep her safe, while making Rudy think she's dead."

Jessie and his crew really didn't have a choice. Jessie had been Rudy's main hit man for over seventeen years. Rudy had come to Jessie three times already wanting Gracie dead. But this fourth time was different. Jessie wasn't sure why he wanted Gracie dead now. He knew both Rudy and Phillip Proctor needed her in order to win the election. He also knew that Rudy had arranged a marriage between Phillip and Gracie. Something wasn't adding up, but Jessie couldn't figure out what it was.

He sat back in his chair with his thumb and forefinger pressing the corners of his eyes, trying to rub out the migraine he had gotten earlier in the day. He racked his brain for the hundredth time going over his last conversation with Rudy trying to find any clues to his murderous motives.

Earlier that night, Jessie met Rudy alone in the parking lot adjacent to the ice cream parlor where Gracie worked. She was working tonight. From Rudy's black Crown Victoria, Jessie watched her smile at the customers, give kids stickers, and laugh with her co-workers.

"Jessie, I've given you three chances to kill my step-daughter," Rudy said. Jessie found a way to make the first carjacking seem like a failed attempt. Jessie had never failed on any hit before. Two more times since then, Rudy came to Jessie about Gracie. Each time, Jessie rigged the outcome so it would appear like a failed attempt.

"I don't know why you refuse to kill the little brat. You've never missed a single hit before." Rudy was fishing for answers, but Jessie wasn't about to divulge anything. He just sat silently in the car, hand resting on the butt of his .38.

Jessie knew why he couldn't kill Gracie. He had fallen in love the second he laid eyes on her five years ago. He had every intention of courting her and making her fall in love with him. Rudy painted her as a stupid girl, believing in love and fairy tales. If that's what Gracie wanted, Jessie planned on giving it to her. But the timing hadn't been right. Now, Jessie was out of time, and he had to take drastic measures to keep her alive.

"Why do you want her dead now? She seems more valuable alive," Jessie asked. He still couldn't figure out Rudy's motives for this murder.

"That's my business," Rudy snapped back. His voice was deep, but there was a demeanor to it that made you cringe. He was seasoned at this type of thing. And he was powerful. Perhaps it was the power behind the voice that made it so menacing. "Do you have any questions? I've given you all the information you need to know."

"No," Jessie replied.

Rudy provided Jessie with everything he needed to know about the shop that couldn't be seen from the outside: the layout in the back stocking area, keys for all the doors and safety vaults, workers' schedules.

"She's cost me two elections, and I'm not going to let her cost me another one. If you can't complete this assignment, then I'm going to have someone else do it and then take care of you in the process," Rudy snarled. "I need her dead!"

"Forgive me, Mr. Talbot, but why did you agree to an arranged marriage between Phillip and Gracie if you're just going to have her killed? Seems to me you would at least wait until after the election or make her Phillip's problem." Jessie desperately searched for Rudy's motive. He needed to know what was behind Rudy's evil mind if he was going to successfully save Gracie.

"Phillip can't handle her. She has impeccable instincts. She's a hard one to deal with. She knows a lot more than I want her to about my business."

Your business is not business. It's killing people,

Jessie thought. He knew Rudy was making excuses and these weren't the true reasons Rudy wanted Jessie to kill her.

"If she refuses to marry Phillip, I have no use for her," Rudy continued.

Jackpot, Jessie thought. Rudy used people and then disposed of them when he had no more use for them. If Gracie wasn't going to help Rudy attain his political power, she was worthless to him.

"What does Phillip think about all this?"

"He doesn't need to know. Make it look like a real robbery and kill her. Everyone knows Gracie puts up a fight. It will not be hard to believe that she gave you a hard time and you had to kill her. Phillip will just move on to the next one."

"But don't you need her to tie your families together to make a stronger political unit?"

Rudy clucked his tongue at Jessie. "My! Aren't we full of questions this evening?"

Jessie knew he hit a raw nerve. He could see it in Rudy's face and body language. It pissed Rudy off that Gracie refused to accept Phillip's hand in marriage. Jessie knew there was more than Gracie's uselessness behind the murder plan. But knowing Rudy, he wasn't going to tell any more.

"Consider it done," Jessie simply stated as he started to exit the car.

Rudy couldn't help himself. He had to make one final threat. Rudy was a smart, manipulative man. He knew there was a reason why Jessie wouldn't kill Gracie. And he speculated it was because Jessie had feelings for the girl.

"If you fail for the fourth time tomorrow night, I will have someone else kill her. Or maybe I'll just have her kidnapped and held hostage in Phillip's apartment. He can use her however he wants her. And we both know how he wants her. Then, I'll come after you. Think carefully, Jessie."

Jessie took deep breaths to try and regain his composure. He opened the car door, slid out, then slammed it shut. He had tried not to let his feelings for Gracie show, but the thought of another man having his way with her was too much for Jessie to handle. It had already been five years since he was in close contact with her.

As Jessie walked away, he could hear Rudy's laughter bellowing out from inside the car.

Jessie climbed into his old rusty gray van with double doors on both the right side and back of the vehicle. He returned to his rental house where he lived with the four other guys that made up his hit crew. The men were close – brothers bonded by secrecy.

When Jessie arrived, his sour mood told the guys everything they needed to know about the meeting with Rudy.

All the guys knew how Jessie felt about Gracie. That became clear soon after they met.

Five years ago on a Saturday afternoon, Jessie and his guys were sitting at an outside table at one of Orlando's local restaurants in the downtown area. Jessie had seen pictures of Gracie before. They were in Rudy's office both at home and at his work. Rudy hated her, but he had an image of a happy family to portray. Jessie thought her beautiful in pictures, but meeting her in person was completely different.

By a stroke of luck, she and some girlfriends sat down at a table next to them.

Jessie walked up to her. He was brazen and he knew it. He was used to being up front and brutally honest.

"Are you Rudy Talbot's daughter?" he asked.

"No!" she quickly countered. "I am not his daughter. I am, unfortunately, his stepdaughter.

There's not much I can do about that. Who are you?" she asked.

"I know your stepfather," Jessie told her.

"I feel sorry for you," Gracie said as she turned away from Jessie.

Jessie walked away from her, but he vowed to himself, from that moment forward to never let anything happen to her. Tomorrow night, he planned to make that promise a reality.

* * *

Shortly after Jessie left the parking lot, Rudy phoned Phillip to arrive in his car with the lights out. Always exactly on time, Phillip got out of his car and into Rudy's.

"All her things have been moved in," Phillip said through grinned teeth. "But she won't even come over to my apartment. She's really starting to piss me off Rudy. I thought you said years ago I'd be able to have her any way I wanted her."

To try to coerce Gracie into a relationship with Phillip, Rudy had her things moved out of her apartment and into Phillip's. But Gracie refused to go there and started living with a friend.

Phillip needed Gracie, more so than Rudy did. The other candidate for senator was a bachelor as well. Survey polls were showing that voters were more likely to select a running mate with a wife. And a beautiful all-American socialite like Gracie Talbot would tip the scales in Phillip's favor.

"Apparently you're not the only one with feelings for Gracie." Rudy put the line out there to see if Phillip would bite. He did.

"Explain," Phillip stated arrogantly.

"Seems my main hit crew's leader has a thing for her."

Phillip sat up even straighter, if that were possible.

"He called me out here tonight to tell me of his plans to rob and then take Gracie for..." he paused a moment to add a dramatic effect to his lie, "personal reasons."

"Like hell!" Phillip spit out. "When is he supposedly doing this?"

Rudy smiled. "His name is Jessie Conners. He's staging a robbery here tomorrow, then abducting Gracie. Ten o' clock pm."

"Conners brought you here and told you about it?"

Rudy didn't say anything. He just let Phillip's mind take him wherever it wanted to go.

"With your permission sir, I'd like to beat him to it. Let me and a few of my men smack her around a little bit. Make her beg to live. Then I should have no problem with her after that. I've got a few tricks up my sleeve," Phillip said. He was as despicable as they came. Corrupt, accepting money for political favors, sleeping around with the local debutantes to gain their votes.

"Well I certainly don't care what you do with the whore, but Conners will. You may have to have him disposed of, if you're catching my drift." Rudy studied Phillip's face for any signs of fear or shock at the request. Rudy had never asked Phillip to murder before. Lie, cheat, steal – yes. Those were the things Phillip was good at. But murder was new to him. However, Rudy was delighted to see Phillip smiling at the idea of killing Conners.

"I have some contacts. I'll take care of Conners and Gracie."

That was exactly what Rudy had hoped Phillip would say. Now he would surely be done with Gracie one way or another. His plan was setting into motion perfectly.

* * *

Phillip was on his cell phone the entire drive back to his apartment. He called his closest accomplice, whom he turned to when it came to dirty dealings. "I need you to find out where a Jessie Conners is living. Then I need you to go there and attach a GPS device to his car. If you find any cell phones, tag 'um. Tomorrow I have to focus on a personal matter, but after that, I'm going to need a way to find Conners and get rid of him. Understand?"

"Yes sir," his accomplice said.

His guy found Conners' place quickly enough. Peering in from across the street, he could see Conners and all his killing buddies gathered around the kitchen table. He quietly ran across the street. Phillip knew he could trust this guy. He had broken into several state officials' offices, rigged elections, and did it all without a trace.

To his surprise, the garage was wide open. He climbed under the old van and attached the GPS tracking device to the chassis just in front of the rear axle. The van itself wasn't locked either, and he was able to go through all the bags, taking inventory of their contents. Jessie had left their unlocked van parked in the open garage so they could load it with the equipment they would need for tomorrow night.

Phillip's guy was shocked by the amount of guns and ammo they had inside the van. He was surprised to find two cell phones charging in the passenger seat. He put bugs in them, and then carefully placed them back where he found them.

Casually walking down the sidewalk, he found a pay phone two blocks down in front of a small convenience store. "It's done," he said to Phillip.

Phillip sat back and smiled. "Come to my apartment. Bring some of your buddies. You know, the ones who do the break-ins with you. We need to talk about Gracie."

Chapter Two

"You going to miss this place? This life?" Clyde asked when they were up and awake the next morning. They had lived in the rental since shortly after the two met that fateful night so many years ago when they were just kids.

The plan was, after getting Gracie in the car, the guys were going to drive over eighteen hours straight to get her to a remote location in the Pocono Mountains in Upstate Pennsylvania. There, at Jessie's cabin, they'd make a life for themselves. All five men and Gracie. Jessie had been planning this since he met her at that restaurant five years ago. After that chance encounter, he bought the cabin hoping to one day keep her safe there. He wasn't going to let anything mess this up.

"No," Jessie said casually. "I'm ready for a fresh start, a new life."

Jessie had been committing murders for the past seventeen years. At first the murders bothered him. But he came from the streets and had seen plenty before he committed his first. By the age of thirteen, both of Jessie's parents had died. He was homeless and would have ended up in one of Orlando's gangs like his cousins if Rudy Talbot hadn't picked him up.

Jessie remembered the day he met Rudy. Sitting outside under the open window of a café in the ghetto district, Jessie could hear a conversation between Rudy Talbot and a local man known on the streets for his murderous ways. The conversation was all about murder, money, and cover-up. Although Clyde was a great shooter and a seasoned killer, he felt uncomfortable with what he was being asked to do. However, Clyde knew the consequences of backing out. He knew of a murder plot by Rudy, and his death was the only thing that Rudy would consider as adequate silencing should he choose not to take the job. The payment would be two million dollars.

In one of his most daring moves ever, Jessie got up, went inside the restaurant to the two men, and pulled up a chair to the table. "Name's Jessie. I just started working with my buddy here. Sorry I'm late. Had some cleaning up to do. Now where were we?"

Jessie had never met either man before. He was gambling that Clyde would accept his help and partnership.

Both men stared in silence at the thirteen-year-old. To give him some credit, he didn't look thirteen. He looked more like fifteen or sixteen. He was big for his age and smarter than anyone gave him credit for. He had the book smarts and an even more keen sense of street smarts. It would prove to become a deadly combination.

Clyde, sitting across from Rudy, finally understood what the kid was doing. He was grateful for the help and hoped he could pass the task off to one of his "workers."

"Well Clyde, you never told me you had hired help now," Rudy finally responded.

"Just switching things up a bit to keep the cops off my tail." Clyde knew Rudy controlled the cops in the city. Still, he always had one eye over his shoulder. You just never knew when Rudy would turn the cops on you, especially if Rudy's name came too close to a murder.

Rudy studied the kid's face. Jessie never took his eyes off of Rudy's. It was challenging and Rudy respected him for that. "What's your name, kid? Where are your parents?"

"Name's Jessie. I don't have any parents."

Rudy's eyebrows shot up. The kid's bluntness and quickness surprised him. All of his clientele knew better than to talk to him like that. He was a man that demanded respect or you would be his next victim. He would just find another guy like Clyde and it would be out with the old and in with the new.

"I see." Rudy took a sip of his coffee while contemplating what to do next. "Can you shoot?"

"Yes."

"Can you shoot well?"

"Yes." Jessie had never held a gun in his life.

"Alright then. I'll leave you and Clyde to iron out the details. Do things as you wish, but remember to tell me when it's taken care of. All the way taken care of." With that, Rudy got up from the table and left, leaving his bill with Clyde and Jessie.

Jessie took Rudy's seat and extended a hand. "Name's Jessie. I was sitting outside and overheard your conversation. For a murder plot, you two didn't seem too concerned about anyone overhearing. Anyway, I think we can help each other out. I need money and some security before one of these street gangs picks me up. Sounds like you need a partner. What do you say?"

Clyde wasn't in a position to turn him down. He was only seventeen himself and started doing jobs for Rudy for the same reason. Word got around in the streets, and if you worked for Rudy Talbot you were respected and left alone to your projects.

Truth was, Rudy was becoming more and more brazen in his requests. Clyde felt uncomfortable with most of them by that point and some were just too difficult for one person to execute. Clyde shook Jessie's hand and smiled. "Welcome aboard."

From that day on, Jessie became the foreman in all the murder operations. Clyde worked out the details, but Jessie was always the one who committed the crime. Eventually, Jessie also became the one who dealt with Rudy. Jessie's talented mind was evident with every assignment he was given. Within the year, Rudy, Jessie, and Clyde had worked out a seemingly nice partnership. And Jessie had become one of Rudy's trusted confidants.

By this point, Jessie had successfully committed so many robberies, he couldn't keep track of the number anymore. Even more disturbing, Jessie had successfully killed and disposed of so many bodies, he couldn't keep track of that number either.

This is why his botched attempts on Gracie's life raised a warning flag with Rudy. Jessie was an accomplished killing machine. There was no reason for Gracie to still be alive, unless Jessie had some ulterior motives he wasn't telling Rudy about.

* * *

Gracie was running late for work. She couldn't find anything she needed. Her stepfather had had all of her belongings moved into Phillip Proctor's apartment. She had told both of them even if hell froze over, she still wouldn't have anything to do with either of them.

Now, she was living out of a friend's house and was frantically searching for her work clothes. Having found them in the dirty laundry pile, Gracie sprayed wrinkle releaser on them. They were going to get wrinkled anyway, she told herself.

Gracie grabbed her purse and keys and opened

the apartment door, running straight into Phillip Proctor's chest.

Phillip grabbed her arms to steady her and didn't let go. Gracie's heart pounded like a drum in her ears.

"Let go of me!" Gracie spat out.

Phillip just pushed her back inside her friend's apartment.

"I see you're staying with friends," Phillip said.

Gracie just stayed silent. She had had one too many encounters with Phillip that ended badly for her. She hoped today was not going to be another.

"You would be much more comfortable with your own things, don't you think?" he asked backing her into a wall. She was pinned between the wall and Phillip, and he still held a tight grip on both her upper arms.

"I'm fine right where I am." She tried to keep her voice even, but she heard it shaking despite her best efforts.

"Yes, I think you are fine right where you are!" Phillip exclaimed with a growing smile on his face.

He pushed his body hard against Gracie. She tried to struggle, but Phillip was a strong man. He frequented the gym daily to keep up his appearance as one of Orlando's most eligible bachelors.

Letting go of one of her arms, Phillip grabbed her cheeks with his hand to hold her head still. At first, he lightly brushed his lips against Gracie's. She felt her heartbeat quicken as she started to panic.

"Let me go!" she screamed at him.

She was too loud. Someone might overhear. Phillip covered her mouth with his hand. She tried pulling it away with her free hand, but Phillip was able to maneuver around to capture both of her wrists behind her back. She was stuck and she knew it.

"Now, that's not any way to talk to your future

husband!" Phillip laughed. "Just think of all the fun we can have together." He took his free hand and rubbed her thigh. She was wearing a jean skirt. It was the standard dress code for the ice cream parlor, but it provided no protection against Phillip. Slowly, he slid his hand up Gracie's skirt and grabbed her butt. Gracie let out a cry that was muffled by the hand over her face.

Phillip moved his hand around to the front of Gracie's panties and lifted the elastic strap just enough to rub one fingertip along the edge. Gracie fought back the tears.

"If you would just cooperate, Gracie, none of this would be so hard on you. You might even enjoy it," Phillip purred into her ear as he put his entire hand below the elastic of her panties, just resting it against the lowest part of her stomach.

Gracie was able to open up her mouth enough to bite Phillip's hand.

"You bitch!" he swore.

Without hesitating, Phillip backhanded Gracie across the face. She cried out in pain.

Pushing her back up against the wall, he reached under her shirt and pulled her bra to the side, taking in a handful of her breast. He covered her mouth with his and kissed her so hard she thought he was going to bust her lips open on the edges of her teeth.

When he finished, Gracie was shaken and crying.

"You will succumb to me. I will have my way with you," Phillip said letting go of her hands. Gracie pushed him away from her.

"Like hell!" she gasped between breaths.

"Let this be a warning. If you don't come to my apartment after work today, I will do much more than what I just did to you. And I will do it over and over again until you decide to cooperate." Phillip turned and walked out the door.

Gracie sank to the floor and wiped at her tears. What choice did she have? She could either be raped by the man or go willingly. And maybe, just maybe, he'd let her come around on her own time.

* * *

The robbery wasn't going to start until ten o' clock pm. It was only two o'clock in the afternoon and everyone was on edge. They knew Rudy would be watching them, and they had to make sure they got Gracie out of there without anyone seeing. They didn't need to pack anything else. Everything was already waiting for them in the Poconos. Besides, anything that looked like it would be missing from their rental house might give them away.

The afternoon passed slowly and the air grew thicker with tension through each hour. By six o'clock, Jessie had walked around the rental house one last time and said a sad goodbye to some of his more treasured items. He was going to miss the continuity of life, but not the dirty jobs he was doing. He was ready for a clean slate. Granted, all the hits he did for Rudy were people that really had it coming to them. Most had committed some type of horrendous crime. Jessie and his gang thought of themselves as people who took the trash out of the world. But the threats to Gracie's life were more than he could handle. He had watched her grow into a beautiful woman over the past five years, watched her laugh, watched her love, and watched her live. He wasn't about to take her life.

Clyde had been right behind him saying his goodbyes to the only life they had ever known. Through the years, he and Clyde had picked up other kids just like themselves. Alone in the world, in need of protection, money, a family. Together, they formed the most infamous, deadly hit crew in the US.

Jessie knew they were early, but the rain clouds were coming in and he decided to head out in case they needed to speed up the robbery due to inclement weather. When they got inside the van, and started to double check their gear, Jessie could feel that something was wrong. He couldn't quite put his finger on it, but something just didn't feel right. One look at Clyde, and he knew Clyde felt it too.

"We need to move earlier," Jessie said. "Something's wrong." They knew to trust Jessie's instincts. He had never been wrong before.

Derek drove the van to the parking lot across the street from the ice cream parlor. Jessie wondered on the way what it was going to be like for Gracie to learn of everything that her stepfather had done; what would it be like for her to leave her mother and little brother behind? To never go home again because she would be raped or killed if she did.

He knew she had an especially close relationship with Timmy, her five-year-old brother. Gracie's mom had fallen under Rudy's spell and was more into the social aspect of being a wealthy man's wife than raising her children. Gracie practically raised herself, and she was raising Timmy. The fact that Rudy hated the relationship between Gracie and Timmy made Jessie nervous for Timmy's safety. But priorities came first, and he had to make sure Gracie was safe before he could even think about her little brother.

So many thoughts and questions were running through his mind. Jessie had patiently waited five years to be with her, which wasn't an easy task for him. Would she be happy with him? Would she settle into a life that she could tolerate? And most important to Jessie, could she love him the way he had loved her since that Saturday afternoon five

years ago? He knew he was just going to have to wait
to find out, but his patience had worn thin.

By eight o'clock, the weather was looking ominous
and the wind blew heavily to the east. Weather like
this in November meant a cold front was coming
through. It wouldn't impact Florida too heavily, but it
stretched up the coast and meant a good amount of
snow on the roads in the Northern states they would
be driving through. It wasn't exactly prime driving
conditions for a getaway after a fake murder and
robbery.

Not only that, but the ice cream shop's dress code
wasn't going to keep Gracie warm in the mountains.
Wearing a jean skirt, white tee-shirt and white
sneakers with no socks, she was going to freeze to
death.

Derek broke the silence. "With this kind of wind,
it's going to be hard to keep the van doors open while
you rob the place and grab the girl. I think we should
go ahead and get ready. I don't want to take any
chances that Rudy will have someone around back
watching. If we hit early, we make our chances of
loosing Rudy even better."

"You're right. It's time," Jessie agreed.

All five guys went about putting on bulletproof
vests under their heavier sweatshirts. They all wore
jeans, gloves, the same size boots, and ski masks to
cover up their identities. All five looked identical. In
all the years they had been doing this, the cops
hadn't come close to finding them. And it helped that
Rudy paid off the police so they wouldn't look into
the matters very far.

It took about twenty minutes to get suited up.
Derek moved back to the driver's seat and put the
van in reverse. He pulled out of the parking lot and
around to the back of the ice cream store. He
stopped and reversed the van, pulling it so close to

the building that when the doors opened up, they hit
the cinderblock wall. No one would see who got in or
out of the van.

* * *

Phillip was feeling quite smug with himself. He was
on an adrenaline high and excited to be included in
the tasks he usually had his subordinates complete.
He couldn't wait to make Gracie beg for him.

He had planned to be waiting in the parking lot of
the Sonic restaurant, next to the back of the ice
cream shop at exactly ten pm. When Gracie left
through the back door, he would be there with his
guys to force her to go with him.

Screw the robbery, he thought. That was more
work than he wanted to do. He'd just go straight to
the source of this whole mess. With a few big guys
around him, he should be very intimidating to her.
She'd have to submit to him. And if she didn't, well,
they would take her back to his place and physically
make her. He told his guys to meet him at his
apartment at nine pm. Phillip would wait until it was
time, then drive to the parking lot behind the store
and wait patiently for Gracie to exit.

* * *

The night had gone fairly quickly for Gracie up until
the rain started. She was able to keep her mind off of
Phillip and just focus on her customers. It was just
past eight thirty and no one seemed to want ice
cream when it was dark, pouring down rain with a
cold wind to go with it.

She was not aware that the backhand Phillip laid
across her cheek was turning colorful shades of blue
and purple. When the customers stopped coming in,

Gracie tried to distract herself by filling up the soft serve machines and toppings, wiping down the tables, and organizing the bowls, cups, and cones.

"Gracie," Emily, her coworker finally said. "What happened to your cheek?"

Gracie was still shaking from her encounter with Phillip.

Gracie sighed and sat down on one of the chairs in the front of the parlor. "That goddamn Phillip Proctor came at me again!" This wasn't the first time he had hit her. It was the first time he had threatened to rape her.

"Gracie, you need to go to the police!" Emily was a good friend and was always so concerned about Gracie.

"My stepfather controls the police. I have to learn to stick up for myself." And tonight, she thought, she was going to have to do a much better job than she did this afternoon.

Gracie stood up and went to work wiping down the rest of the tables in the front parlor area. As she finished, she headed into the back room to dump out and refill her water bucket. She stopped cold in her tracks when she heard Emily scream and the door slam open against the glass storefront.

Everything happened so quickly, Gracie wasn't sure what happened in what particular order. She heard Emily's scream, the door slam, and a man shout, "Everyone get on the floor!" It wasn't Phillip. That much she was able to comprehend.

The door was five feet directly in front of the opening to get behind the counter. She was crouched just behind the counter top. It suddenly occurred to her that she was only five feet away from the gunman with nothing there to protect her. She wasn't sure if she made the conscious decision to get up and run to the back of the store, or if her body made the decision for her, but she felt herself running as fast as she could. Gunshots rang out making Gracie and her other coworkers scream.

Jessie cursed under his breath. He was too jumpy and didn't mean to hit the trigger. He fired too early. But he knew his guys would know that, and was glad Gracie ran to the back room. She was safest there, out of the site of Rudy. Jessie would bet money that he was watching.

Gracie stopped as she turned the corner to the back storage room. Two more men were entering through the back door. She heard footsteps quickly approaching her from behind as she tried to duck under the countertop in the back room.

A hand grabbed her arm and forced her to keep moving without allowing her to look back. She didn't have time to struggle. Soon, she and her co-workers were pushed to a corner in the back room next to the freezers, out of sight of the front of the store. Everyone else had their heads down and were hysterical. Gracie was dry-eyed, watching the masked gunmen. She couldn't believe she was being attacked a second time in one day.

Gracie had terrible asthma and the stress from her altercation with Phillip, plus the fear from the robbery, had triggered an attack. She knew she needed to stay calm and collected or she'd go into a panic and loose consciousness, and probably be shot to death. She needed to get to her purse, which was under the cash register in the front of the store.

She waited until two of the men were breaking into the safe and the two that entered through the front of the door passed them in the corner to securely prop open the back door. Everything blurred together after that. She made a break for it to get to her purse. She got to the open doorway between the back room and the front of the store. A very strong,

very powerful hand gripped her arms, swung her
around hitting her back against the wall. She was
face to face with him. The second time today she
found herself pushed up against a wall by a man.

All she could see was his eyes. He had beautiful
eyes for such an evil man. They were a deep blue,
not like her crystal blue. But there was something
haunting in them. It was like they were trying to tell
her something, but she didn't know what. This time,
she struggled, but his hands were firm. She was
planted exactly where she was standing.

"Boss, we're out! Let's go!" Clyde yelled.

Jessie looked at Gracie and whispered close to her
ear "Don't fight me. Trust me." He pulled back and
stared into her eyes once again. Jessie knew that if
Rudy was spying on their operation, he would be
able to see Jessie with Gracie.

Everything in Gracie's body was telling her to fight
until she was shot dead. She wasn't about to let
what happened this afternoon happen again tonight.
And she needed her inhaler. She could see her bag
with her inhaler inside from where Jessie had her
pinned.

"I need to get my things!" she yelled.

"Walk!" he demanded.

Gracie just stared at him for another second. She
couldn't believe she was still alive at twenty-six. She
was surprised Rudy hadn't killed her himself by now.
She thought she might not make it past twenty-six
after all.

But there was something about the way he said
"trust me" that made her stand completely still.

He kept his hand firmly wrapped around her right
upper arm, and directed her to the back door. She
expected to be tied up with the rest of her co-
workers, but was forced to walk directly pass them.
The wind and rain hit her face instantly as she was

forced outside, soaking her in a matter of seconds. It was cold and the rain came down with such force it stung her face. Pushing her into the back of the van, the doors slammed shut and the van took off.

Looking behind her, Gracie expected to see her co-workers in the van. That's when the true terror struck. She was all alone with five masked gunmen.

Chapter Three

"Keep your head down. Lay on the floor until I tell you to get up," the guy with the deep blue eyes ordered. From what she gathered, he was the one in charge.

It had taken them a total of six minutes to complete the robbery and abduct Gracie.

Rudy watched from across the street. "Damn it!" he yelled. They were early. Too early. "Get Phillip on the phone now!" he ordered his driver.

After two rings, Phillip answered. "Get to the store now!" Rudy ordered. "Conners moved in early. He's got Gracie. You idiot! You were supposed to beat him to it or have him taken care of!"

Phillip was furious, but confident he'd eventually get Gracie. Conners and his crew had no idea they were being tracked. Phillip turned on the tracking device and saw them heading away from the store.

"I had a GPS installed on their van last night. I'll head out with a few of my guys and chase them down," Phillip said too casually for Rudy's liking.

"And what makes you think that Conners will just hand her over to you?" Rudy nervously asked. Gracie was in the hands of one of the most infamous organized crime hit team leaders. She was as good as gone. Phillip was no match for the likes of Conners and his crew. But Phillip was too arrogant to think that.

"We'll figure it out," Phillip quickly said. He was used to sweet-talking his way through life. He figured he'd casually approach the guy and strike some kind of a deal. Women were, after all, property and nothing that money couldn't buy.

Phillip called his guys and within a few minutes, they were on the trail of Conners and his crew. They were about thirty minutes behind them. His driver hit the gas, as they tried to catch up with them.

* * *

"Boss, I bet he's having us followed. I thought I saw Rudy's car when we pulled out from behind the shop. He's going to think something's up because we moved in early." Derek never missed a trick. He was an excellent driver who had an eye for detail. "I'm gonna start taking a few back roads. Something's just making me very uncomfortable." Just like Jessie's instincts were to be trusted on a hit, Derek's were to be trusted when it came to driving and covering their tracks.

The air was now even thicker with tension. Had they really just pulled off the rescue of Gracie Talbot? But what was wrong with her? She was shaking and sweating. She seemed like she didn't even have the energy to sit up, let alone fight back. Jessie swore he had never abducted anyone as compliant as Gracie was.

She tried to keep her eyes open, but struggled. She tried to focus on him, but he seemed to be a blur with the ski mask on. Jessie could tell she was looking solely at him. He took off his mask, hoping she might calm down.

Gracie was shocked again. The "boss" was actually handsome. He had dark brown, wavy hair that was long enough to touch his shoulders. He was tan with high cheekbones, and those deep piercing blue eyes. He took off his sweatshirt which was still soaked by the rain to unveil the bulletproof vest he had on underneath. But even the bulky vest couldn't hide that he was extremely muscular. She had never seen anyone that was so menacing and good-looking at the same time. He would have been the dictionary's picture of a bad-boy-all-grown-up if it had one. But her attraction to him did no good in her particular situation. She needed her inhaler, or she would die.

"Gracie, we're not going to hurt you."

Yeah right, she thought! How many times have they said that to someone right before they killed them? And how the hell does he know my name?

Everyone in the car was quiet, except for Derek, the driver, who swore every few minutes.

"Who are you?" she managed to squeak out.

"I'm Jessie. This is Clyde, Bubba, Peter, and that man driving is Derek."

She shook her head. "You don't understand. It hurts to talk. I need my inhaler. I can't breathe."

Jessie's face turned white. Rudy never told him about her asthma. He had never seen her use an inhaler in all the times he was watching her. It dawned on him that Rudy purposefully left out that one very crucial piece of information.

"Bastard!" The rest of the guys were taking off their ski masks.

"We can't go back," Derek said. "Something's off about this whole thing." Jessie knew Derek was right because he could feel it too.

"If I don't get my inhaler, I'll die," Gracie said as she started to slip away into an unconscious sleep. It occurred to her that was probably what these guys wanted. They probably had a score to settle with Rudy and she was the bargaining chip. Or maybe Rudy simply paid them to dispose of her. Well, she'd help them out and just slip off into the darkness.

"Stay awake!" Jessie shouted at her. She could feel him shaking her shoulders, and she managed to open her eyes one more time before she allowed herself to slip into a deep unconscious sleep, barely able to breathe.

When she woke up, they were still on the road. She wasn't sure how long she was unconscious. Wrapped up in blankets with a pillow under her head, Jessie was sitting next to her. She could hear them talking, formulating another plan.

Gracie needed an inhaler and they had to find one. The only option at that point was another robbery. Derek found on his GPS system all the twenty-four hour pharmacies in Jacksonville. They had gotten off I-10 and were in the heart of Jacksonville looking for the largest pharmacy to rob. The larger the pharmacy, the better the chance of finding Gracie's medication, they thought.

Jessie looked down and found her struggling to keep breathing. She was wheezing and he knew she didn't have much time.

He shook her hard, hard enough for her to open her eyes. "What is the name of your medicine?" he asked her. He had a quick, abrupt way of speaking. There was no fooling around with this guy.

She opened her mouth but nothing came back. She started to slip back into unconsciousness, but Jessie grabbed her shoulders and shook her.

"Stay awake!" he shouted at her. "What medicines do you need?" He tried propping an arm behind her to get her to sit up slightly to stay awake. It seemed to help.

Gracie swallowed. Were they actually trying to help her? She could have sworn they were going to kill her. And if that was the case, she would rather just curl up in an unconscious asthma attack and die.

She forced herself to talk. "Nebulizer machine with steroids." She swallowed hard. "Albulterol inhaler." Swallowed again and started wheezing at the effort it took to talk and push air in and out of her lungs. "Prednisone, 10 days." She started coughing and was slipping back into oblivion. "Oxygen."

Bubba had it all written down. When they found the pharmacy, everyone suited up again for the second robbery of the night. Derek stayed with the car and watched Gracie. If this went as planned, they should be back in the van in no longer than three minutes.

Four masked gunmen stormed the Walgreens. Two stayed by the front door, the other two ran to the back pharmacy. Running on pure adrenaline, Jessie kicked down the door leading into the pharmacy department, and had the workers lined up with their hands up against the back wall within a matter of seconds. He grabbed the head pharmacist by the arm and turned her around. "I need these. You have two minutes, or I shoot." His voice was low, deep, and he meant what he said. He just left out the part that he wasn't planning on shooting anyone.

The pharmacist was quick, but not quick enough. Jessie nodded to Clyde. He shot three rounds into the air. Jessie started making his way through the aisles, finding what Gracie needed.

Waiting in the car, Derek had a chance to think about his uneasy feeling. Then it hit him. They were probably being tracked and followed.

He swore like a drunken sailor, jumped out of the van, and crawled underneath it with a flashlight. It took him less than five seconds to find the attached GPS system. Whoever attached it to the car did a really poor job at hiding it. Regardless, they were being tracked and Derek didn't think they had much time until they were found. They were just sitting in a parking lot. He returned to the driver's seat with the other GPS system in his hand. He would have to throw off whoever was tracking them.

After five agonizing minutes, Derek was relieved to see all four of his guys run back out of the store. He opened up the back door of the van for them as they piled inside.

Derek stayed at the back of the van with one door propped open. "Why aren't you driving?" Jessie yelled at him. He didn't yell at his guys, but this was so unusual for Derek to be anywhere besides the driver seat.

"Some asshole attached a GPS to us. That's what's going on. I found it under the van. Stay here! I'll be right back!" Derek jumped out of the van with his ski mask still on. He ran to the closest vehicle, a Ford Ranger. Whoever was following them would end up following the White Ranger.

* * *

Phillip and a few of the guys he recruited to do the brunt of his dirty work had been tracking Conners' van from Orlando to Jacksonville. "Mr. Proctor, they seem to have stopped," his driver informed him.

"Where?" Phillip asked, sitting forward, peering through the windows that opened up into the front seat.

"At a Walgreens."

"Why the hell would they do that?" he asked. "How far away are we?"

His driver checked the GPS. "About twenty minutes."

Phillip swore under his breath. "Let's hope they stay for a while. Drive faster!" Phillip ordered. He sat, trying to figure out how he was going to sweet talk his way to Gracie. Phillip thought Jessie obviously had not been around her enough. How could anyone want Gracie enough to go to this much trouble?

Every five minutes, Phillip's driver informed Jessie that the GPS was still at Walgreens. He was baffled why they would be spending this much time there. Soon enough, they drove down the street the store was on. To their surprise, they found it blocked off with the police directing traffic in the opposite direction.

"What the hell is going on here?" Phillip demanded. He had his driver pull up to the police officer.

"Name's Phillip Proctor, Senator Proctor's son. What seems to be going on tonight?" His smile was all charm and concern. The officer fell right into his trap.

As he waved a few other cars around Proctor's, he informed him that the Walgreens had been robbed by four gunmen, all wearing ski masks. "We just got in a report that a group of men matching their very description may have robbed a store in Orlando."

"What kind of store?" Phillip was going to pry every little piece of information out of the officer. It was one of his specialties.

"An ice-cream parlor," the officer said, directing another car around Phillip's.

"Why would anyone rob an ice-cream parlor in Orlando, then a Walgreens in Jacksonville?" he probed.

The officer looked around, making sure his superiors didn't hear him giving out information. "Word at the station is that some guys have it out for running mate Rudy Talbot, and abducted his daughter. We think they're trying to keep her alive because they only stole her medication. We're expecting to get a ransom letter or call any time now."

That was the information Phillip wanted to know – if Gracie was alive or dead. Apparently, they were trying to keep her alive. Phillip wanted her alive and he wanted her to be with him. His blood boiled at the thought of her being someone else's property. Surely if this Conners guy could keep her against her will, Phillip could too. He couldn't see any reason why anyone would want to be with a cold-blooded killer over him, really anyone over him.

Maybe this would give Gracie a taste of her own medicine. If she thought that life would be so bad with him, let her experience life with men who killed for a living. Then she would come running to him. Phillip just knew it. Maybe it wasn't such a bad thing Gracie was with Conners for a little while. He just had to make sure he didn't let her stay too long. Elections were coming up soon, and he would get more votes if Gracie showed up by his side right before elections. Suddenly, Phillip didn't feel so frustrated with the situation.

"Here's my card," Phillip said handing the police officer his business card out of his jacket, along with a thousand dollar bill. "I'll make sure it's worth your while to keep me in the loop. It's a bit of a personal matter where Ms. Talbot's concerned."

"Sure thing, Mr. Proctor," the officer said, casually tucking the card and money into his pocket.

His driver pulled away and rolled up the window for Phillip. "Mr. Proctor?" his driver asked.

"What?" Phillip snapped back annoyed that his driver had the nerve to interrupt the new plan he was formulating in his mind.

His driver looked nervously in the rearview mirror. "The tracking system is still at Walgreens."

Phillip didn't see what this had to do with anything. "And...," he inquired further.

"Conners obviously isn't at Walgreens. Either the GPS system fell off or they found it and did something with it. We have no way of knowing where they are now."

Phillip was feeling pretty smug until then. How would he track Gracie and get her back if he didn't know where she was? He cursed, and hit the side of his fist against the window. He cursed again at the pain he felt when he made contact with the glass. Conners won again. He'd be damned if he was going to lose next time. He would find Gracie and she would be his.

Chapter Four

After Derek had secured the GPS to the White Ford Ranger, they were back on the road. It occurred to Jessie that the robbery at Walgreens for those specific items just gave away the fact that they were trying to keep Gracie alive. Usually he killed his victims immediately and then dumped the bodies. Rudy would be suspicious and Jessie would have to come up with a way to make Rudy think he killed her. But right now, Jessie needed to figure out how to give Gracie her meds. She was completely unconscious and her breathing was shallow. Her skin was pale and gray with beads of sweat across her forehead. She was dead cold to the touch.

Jessie wrapped the blankets tighter around her. She was completely soaked by the rain, and he feared she was becoming hypothermic. To make matters worse, the van had no heat. It was a damp, rainy, cold November.

Usually cool, calm, and collected, Jessie was in a panic.

"What do we do first?" he asked Clyde. Clyde always knew what to do when Jessie didn't.

"Let's put the oxygen mask on her while we figure out the rest of these meds."

Jessie took great care in gently lifting her head to attach the mask. They turned on the oxygen, and then turned their attention to figuring out the rest of her medication.

"She said she needed her inhaler. Let's try to get a couple puffs in her," Clyde suggested. Jessie gently removed the mask and forced her mouth slightly open to place the inhaler just inside her lips. He had never noticed her lips before, not in this way at least. But at that moment, he wanted to kiss her. Instead, he gave her four puffs from her inhaler with each breath she struggled to breathe in. At the last puff, Gracie started coughing and lifted her arm, wrapping her hand around Jessie's hand. He tried to take his away, but Gracie kept it where it was. So he gave her two more puffs when she inhaled. That was enough for her to open her eyes again.

She lowered her hand, and Clyde handed Jessie the nebulizer machine he had put together while Jessie gave her puffs of her inhaler. When she was finally able to focus her eyes again for a second time, she could see a breathing machine strapped to her face. They were giving her medications. Leaning over her, Jessie held the mask over her mouth and nose so it didn't slip off when the van hit rough roads.

He had one arm braced on the far side of her and was sitting on the other. He didn't want to get too close to her and make her more frightened, but he knew she needed body heat. So he stayed close. Gracie wasn't awake long. Just long enough to get a smile from him. But that effort was enough to send her into her second unconscious sleep.

* * *

Days could have passed for all she knew. Gracie remembered dreaming, or at least she thought she was dreaming, about a robbery at the ice cream store. Lying on the floor of a van with five masked gunmen. Rain and bright lights peering in at her through windows of a moving vehicle.

Jessie and his guys took turns driving straight through the night and into the next day. They took I-95 North until they reached the Pennsylvania turnpike. From there, they headed towards the Pocono Mountains. Once they were within an hour of Jessie's cabin, the conversation started to pick up again. He checked on Gracie. She was sound asleep. Her breathing was much better, although still a little heavier-sounding than he would have liked.

"Alright guys," Jessie said. "Things didn't go exactly as planned. Rudy's going to want to know what happened."

Jessie paused for a moment, looking down at Gracie again. "I think it's time we stopped reporting to Rudy and prepare for a fight." Jessie knew if they stopped working for Rudy, he'd find a new group of guys to find and kill them. All of them.

"We have the upper hand," he continued. "My cabin's in one of the most remote locations in the mountains. There are five of us. And I can always call on my cousins for reinforcements. Rudy has no idea that I have this cabin. It's big enough for all of us. I say we stay here in the mountains and make a life for ourselves. I think it's time to settle down." With that last statement, he looked down at Gracie.

If Bubba was good for one thing, it was playing devil's advocate. "Boss, we could still report to him and tell him our dumping site had some issues and that we needed to keep Gracie alive until we found a new one."

Typically the guys headed west towards Texas where there was a lot of new construction. They would wait until concrete was being poured for a large building, sneak onto the construction site at night, and dump the body into the concrete. It was disturbing the amount of buildings that were built on top of dead bodies.

"It would take them a while to find us," Peter said.

"But this is going to be all over the news! First a robbery and abduction of Gracie Talbot. Not just any girl, but Rudy Talbot's daughter. Then a second robbery in Jacksonville for her specific medications. It shows we're headed north. We left a really easy track to follow. And if they post Gracie's picture on the TV or anywhere in the media, everyone is going to know it's her. No one can pass off for Gracie." Clyde was right. They practically left breadcrumbs behind, and the abduction was probably all over the news. If the van had a radio, which it didn't, they were sure they would hear about it on there.

"If we settle down, Gracie's going to have to agree to a lot of things. I think we should wait until she wakes up and we can talk to her about the different options. In the meantime, I'm with Clyde. I think we should keep in contact with Rudy so he doesn't suspect anything unusual right away. It gives us time to get settled in the cabin." Derek was right.

Finally, Jessie gave in. "Ok, we'll see what Gracie wants to do once she wakes up. I'll keep up all the false pretenses with Rudy in the mean time. We need to stop at a pay phone."

They pulled over about thirty minutes away from their cabin. Jessie knew he had to keep the conversation under a minute, or it could be traced. He called Rudy's private number to his home office and waited for him to answer.

Jessie hoped he could keep his voice steady like all their other conversations.

"You jumped the gun," Rudy answered, letting Jessie know that he was right. Rudy was watching them at the ice cream shop. "Seems like the little bitch gave you a hard time."

Jessie knew all too well how Rudy tried to keep

you on the phone to find out your exact location.

"Can't talk now, but everything's taken care of. Had to switch things up a bit. I'll explain more later."

"I want to know now."

"Not a good place for that." Jessie hoped he could get away with pretending he was in a populated area and couldn't be overheard. "It's done," he repeated. "I have to go." Jessie hung up the phone. They were approaching a minute. He hoped his bluntness, which he usually kept aside when dealing with Rudy, didn't tip Rudy off any.

Derek drove the last stretch of the drive, up the winding, snowy roads with caution. The van was sliding everywhere and Jessie had to lean over Gracie and press both arms around her to keep her from rolling around on the floorboard. Finally, they saw it.

Earning a few million dollars for a couple of hits a year will buy you a lot of things. For Jessie, it bought a remotely located log cabin. It was the perfect size for a large family. With four large bedrooms, three bathrooms, a den area, living room, dining area, kitchen, basement, and two balconies, it provided enough space for five large men. The inside was very rustic, yet cozy. Every room had a fireplace with hearth and mantel. Wooden beams spanned over the vaulted living room ceiling, the same as was in the master bedroom upstairs.

The cabin sat up high on the mountain, looking down around three sides and out towards a lake on the fourth. That was one of the exact reasons he had picked this cabin. It was like a natural fortress. With heavy foliage around all sides and great vantage points, he couldn't find a better fort if he had built it himself.

The property was remarkable. The lake was not too far off the back of the house. That would serve him nicely should he need to get away by boat, which he had in the boathouse on the shore. A large detached garage at the front of the property housed all of Jessie's vehicles. He kept a black Tahoe, fueled up and packed with basic necessities should Jessie and his crew need to quickly escape. There was also a stable should he ever choose to get horses. And the entire property was guarded by a large, ten-foot-tall metal gate. Total, the property contained just over ten acres. Jessie also liked the idea of his guys building cabins on the outskirts. They were a family and family stayed close.

Since he bought the cabin five years ago, Jessie had used it as a getaway between jobs. Settling down with Gracie was all he could think of. It was the perfect spot for her. No one would know where they were. Now she was finally here, in the Poconos with him at his cabin.

As they pulled up the drive, the tension in the air thinned out. Brear and Honey, Jessie's two Bernese Mountain dogs ran outside through the doggie door to greet them. Jessie never knew who was happier to see each other – the dogs to see him, or him to see the dogs.

They opened the van doors, and Jessie lifted Gracie into him arms. Brear sniffed at her. Gracie was still wrapped up in thick blankets, making it awkward to carry her. He took her inside, walking between the kitchen to his right and dining area to his left, through the living room straight in front of him, and up the stairs on the far right of the living room.

"Bubba, why don't you help me get Gracie settled?" Jessie called, as he was halfway up the stairs.

Bubba was black, tall, and overly muscular. Yet he was a gentle giant and knew how to put everyone at ease in any situation. Gracie was still sleeping, but Jessie knew she would be drawn into a close friendship with Bubba. Bubba was also going to be assigned to Gracie as her personal bodyguard.

When he got her into his bedroom, Jessie immediately laid her down on the bed. Bubba went straight to the fireplace. Brear and Honey followed. Jessie removed all the blankets around Gracie and found that the blankets actually kept Gracie's clothes from drying. Her clothes were still wet from the previous night. "Damn," he let out under his breath.

"What's wrong, boss?" Bubba asked.

"She's still soaking wet from last night. The blankets didn't let her dry, and she's dead cold."

"You need to warm her up. Either put her in the bath tub with warm water, or lie next to her and let your body heat warm her up." Bubba was good with health information. He was the type of guy who looked like he knew nothing, yet knew every bit of information you thought you'd never need to know. "But you have to strip off her clothes, Boss. She can't stay in them."

Jessie was afraid of that. He was afraid of the way she made him feel. Afraid he couldn't keep his feelings in check. Afraid that she would reject him outright. Afraid he might lose her to the cold.

He contemplated which option would be best, and decided to strip her of her wet clothes, put one of his flannel button-down shirts on her, and climb into bed next to her. He didn't think he could handle seeing her naked in the bathtub, and he realized he was exhausted now that he had time to think about it.

Bubba was still working on the fire and Jessie removed both her shoes. Peter's voice came bellowing up from downstairs. "Boss, you're going to want to hear this!"

"Not now!" Jessie snapped back.

"Really, Boss! Rudy's all over the TV pleading for any information about the abductors who took his daughter," Peter shouted back.

"Damn!" Jessie let out again. It was proving to be his favorite word. Bubba turned from a flaming fire toward Jessie and Gracie.

"You just worry about the girl right now, Boss," Bubba said.

You could hear the wind howling past the doors and windows. The second part of the cold front was sweeping across the Eastern seaboard and it was expected to be worse than the first. Jessie was glad the cabin would protect them from this round of storms.

Bubba left and Jessie started the task of removing Gracie's clothes. He first grabbed a flannel out of his drawer, then unbuttoned her skirt and slid it down over her legs. Even though she was of average size for her height, her legs seemed to go on forever. He was careful not to disturb her too much when he took off her soaked white t-shirt. Because it was wet, he could see right through it. But it was different when she wasn't wearing it at all. Finally, he took off her bra and panties. He tried not to look at her like that, but he couldn't help himself.

She was beautiful. Her skin was light ivory with freckles across her shoulders and chest. She was muscular. Her body was more sculpted than he had imagined. In the past, he would lie in bed and think about what Gracie would look like out of her clothes. But having her here in his bed, naked, made his blood boil.

Quickly, before he did something he would later regret, or Gracie would kill him for, he put his flannel on her and buttoned it up. He then positioned her in bed and piled blankets and comforters around her for warmth.

He hung her clothes in the bathroom to dry, then headed downstairs for a quick glance at the TV to see what Rudy was up to. He descended the stairs and heard the pathetic excuse for a grieving stepfather before he could see him on TV.

Rudy was holding a handkerchief, as if he'd actually been crying. He had the Orange County Police Chief on one side of him and his Catholic priest on the other. Rudy certainly had connections in Florida.

First, the Police Chief made a brief statement. "We received a ransom letter via fax directly to Mr. Talbot shortly after these men committed a second robbery in Jacksonville. They are asking for ten million dollars and for Mr. Talbot to step out of the running for State Attorney General. We believe that these men are keeping Gracie Talbot alive at this time. This is still a search and rescue mission. We are asking for the safe return of Ms. Talbot. In exchange, the men who took Gracie will only receive the minimum sentence for their crime if they return her alive."

Rudy kept his face down to hide the expression on his face. He wasn't crying, but occasionally blotted at the corners of his eyes as if he were. He was a masterful actor. But to Jessie, he was just plain pathetic.

"I'd like to make a plea to the men who took my daughter. She's a good girl. She's never been in any trouble. Her mother is so sick over this she's in the hospital. We'll gladly pay you your ransom fee if you would safely return her to us." Rudy turned away from the camera like the statement was emotionally too much for him to handle. Jessie hissed under his breath when all five of their pictures flashed across the screen. Rudy gave them up.

The Police Chief continued. "These are the five men that have been identified by the workers at both the ice cream parlor where Gracie was abducted and the Walgreens that was later robbed. If you have any information, please call the number on the bottom of your screen. These men are considered armed and dangerous. Do not try to approach them yourself. All tips will remain anonymous and will be thoroughly looked into."

The Catholic priest moved closer to the microphone. "Let's all join in prayer." That was all Jessie was willing to listen to.

"Turn that crap off," Jessie said with a sharp tone to his voice. "Rudy's obviously turned on us. Why?" he asked himself out loud.

"How did we mess up so bad? He had this whole thing figured out. He threw us under the bus. This means he's got another hit team already, had them before we even took Gracie. And we thought we were the only one. Who knows how many hit teams Rudy actually has! I knew he was slime, but I never imagined he would stoop this low," Peter exclaimed.

"There's something more behind this." Clyde spoke the exact words Jessie was thinking. "He doesn't care about Gracie. We know that. Why would he want her back? There's another component to this that we don't know about yet."

"I think it's safe to assume that Clyde's right," Jessie confirmed. "We need to keep our heads down and stay vigilant. The other hit crew was tracking us. Hopefully we lost them in Jacksonville. Let's rest up the next couple of days and see how this whole thing unfolds." Everyone agreed. Jessie left the room and headed back upstairs.

There was more to this and Jessie knew it. Rudy didn't care if Gracie was alive or dead. So why would he have someone following them? Why was he watching the ice cream shop earlier in the night than their original hit was scheduled? Was someone else supposed to show up? And why would he make a public statement wanting her back? Things weren't adding up. Maybe he was just too tired to see it all clearly.

He quietly opened the bedroom door, careful to not wake Gracie. Quickly crossing the room, he stood next to her side of the bed. He put a hand on her forehead to see if she had warmed up at all, but she was still deathly cold. She needed his body heat to warm up. There was no way around it. As much as he wanted to get close to her, he never imagined the first time he held Gracie would be when she was seemingly unconscious and fighting hypothermia. But at this point, he didn't care. He just wanted her alive.

He crossed the room, to the other side of the bed. Then, he stripped down to his boxers, and crawled in bed next to her. Pulling her tightly against him, he made his body fold directly into every curve of hers. She was facing him, and he couldn't help but brush a tendril of hair across her forehead and then kiss her there. Jessie was asleep in a matter of seconds with Gracie locked tightly in his arms.

Chapter Five

When she awoke, Gracie was lying in a bed with a man that she swore was trying to kill her. She was under heavy blankets in an oversized man's flannel shirt with no underwear. His arms were wrapped around her so tight, she couldn't even wiggle her way out of his hold.

She was delirious and scared. She had never seen this room before. Lying still to not wake him, Gracie took in her surroundings while contemplating her next move. The door leading out of the room was directly in the middle of the opposite wall. A dresser with a mirror was to the left of it, a bookshelf to the right. On the right side of the room was another door that appeared to open into a bathroom and closet. To the left of her was a fireplace, blazing with a hot fire, and two French doors on either side, covered in thick white fabric. The fireplace was made out of gray stone, with a mantel and hearth. Wooden beams streamed along the vaulted ceiling making the room feel warm and cozy. The walls were painted a deep amber. Quite simply, the room was beautiful.

At first she didn't see the two Bernese Mountain Dogs that were sleeping in front of the fireplace. Her efforts to wiggle herself free must have disturbed them from their slumber. Slowly, she placed one of Jessie's arms on his side. She was even more cautious not to wake him when she lifted herself up

and scooted over to the other side of the bed. The
dogs were excited to see her. She smiled at them.
She loved dogs. They seemed to understand she was
weak and scared, but still ran over to her and put
their heads on her lap. The larger of the two, a male
she presumed, wagged his tail with enthusiasm.

She scratched behind their ears and started to
become aware how sick she actually was. Breathing
took more effort than she had. Sitting up made her
lightheaded. Her throat burned. While taking a deep
breath, she coughed.

Covering her mouth, she couldn't keep her
coughing from waking Jessie. He opened his eyes
and quickly sat up. Grabbing something off the
nightstand, he handed it to her. It was her inhaler.
She instinctively took it from him and inhaled two
puffs. After her coughing seemed to calm down, she
stared at him.

"You had us all a little scared there for a while,"
he said. His voice was deep, but kind. Different than
the way he spoke to her in the ice cream parlor.

Gracie just peered at him over the covers. She felt
uncomfortable sitting in a bed with him, in only a
shirt. It was just the two of them and two frisky dogs
in a bedroom.

"I want to go home," she said. The effort to say
those few words turned into another coughing fit,
followed by two more puffs on her inhaler.

Jessie shook his head and sat on the same edge of
the bed, petting the calmer of the two dogs.

"You can't," he replied quickly. "If you go home,
you're as good as dead."

"I don't understand."

"I'll explain it all to you. But you're safe here. I
won't let anything happen to you."

"You almost killed me!" she shot back. Her voice
was raspy.

"I know and I'm sorry. I thought I had everything covered. I never meant for that to happen. You don't like to let people know your weak side, do you?" In all the hours he'd spent watching Gracie, never once did she use her inhaler.

Gracie couldn't stop coughing now. She needed more than just her inhaler. It usually took days for her to regain normal breathing patterns after an attack that bad. She knew she needed to take it easy. But she didn't know what these guys had planned for her. She was terrified.

Jessie got her nebulizer machine out, put it on her mouth, and helped her lie back down. She didn't want to lie in bed with someone who was going to hurt her. She was already wearing his clothes. Had he done something to her while he was undressing her? She didn't know. She didn't think so. Nonetheless, she fought him this time.

"Damn it, Gracie, just lay down!" he yelled out of frustration.

She kept trying to swing her legs around the edge of the bed, but even that wasn't happening very quickly. She was just too weak. She managed to brush off his hand holding the medicine mask over her face. She threw the covers back and sat up, then stood for the first time in almost twenty-four hours. Maybe she stood up too quickly, or she was just that sick, but after two steps, she started to sway. Black and white spots blurred her vision and her ears began to ring. She felt him pick her up, and put her right back into the bed. Then, he fastened the breathing machine to her face, and wrapped his arms around her once again, assuring that she was not getting away.

"Gracie, I am not going to hurt you. You need to calm down. Right now, just trust me that I won't hurt you," Jessie pleaded.

This time, Gracie didn't fight it. He felt good, too good really. His body fit every curve of hers. Not like Phillip, who forced himself against her curves. Jessie seemed to naturally fit into her curves. And he was warm. She was chilled to the bone and he was so warm. And for some unknown reason, her instincts told her to trust him. Her instincts kept her alive from Rudy for twenty-six years, so she wasn't about to turn against them now. She settled down, and couldn't help herself from nudging closer to him. It finally occurred to her that he was wearing nothing more than boxer shorts and she was in nothing more than a flannel shirt. It nearly killed him, but he stayed decent and didn't seem to be interested in taking advantage of her.

* * *

Rudy Talbot sat in his office with Senator Proctor and his son Phillip. Senator Proctor and Rudy had been confidants to each other for over forty years. Rudy had put on a good show for the press today. And his wife had been so grief-stricken, he had her hospitalized so he wouldn't have to deal with her. Timmy, their five-year-old son hadn't said one word since his sister was abducted. The mansion's staff of nannies were making sure he was kept inside, out of the public's eye, per Rudy's request. He wanted to appear like a heartbroken father afraid for his remaining child.

"You're sure they're keeping her alive?" Rudy asked Phillip.

"I don't know one hundred percent, but I'd bet my life on it," Phillip replied.

"That's not something I'd wager very often my friend," Rudy said with a smirk. "For your sake, I hope you're right. Now, where would he take her?"

Rudy was smart and manipulative, but not as smart as he wanted you to think.

"Well, they usually go west. This time, they robbed a store in Jacksonville, which makes me think they're going north. Then we've had some tips come in that the van was spotted at a rest stop as far north as DC. Where north they are headed, I don't know yet. But I'll find out." Phillip was able to find out any information he wanted from the police officer he met the previous night in Jacksonville. Any tips that came in went to Phillip first, then to the rest of the officers on the case.

"Yes, let's bet on your life that you do!" Rudy abruptly got out of his office chair and waited for the Senator and Phillip to leave his office. He had a long day of faking grief and making pleas of help to the public. He needed his rest if he was going to keep up this charade.

* * *

Jessie and Gracie both slept through the night. Jessie was the first one to wake the next morning. He slowly slid out of bed, put on a pair of jeans and made his way down the stairs and into the kitchen. Everyone was already awake and scattered throughout the kitchen and dining area, talking about their predicament.

"Morning," he said casually. All eyes were on him. It wasn't surprising. He had just slept through the night with Gracie Talbot in his bed. It had been a long time since they had a girl with them. And they had never had a girl with them that their boss was blindly in love with. Jessie knew they wanted to know more than "morning." But he wasn't one to oblige others of his own personal business. And where Gracie was concerned, that was personal business.

"Morning," most said back to him.

"So fill me in. How bad has it gotten?" Jessie asked, leaning his back against the kitchen countertop.

Clyde broke the news. "Pretty bad. He put Gracie's mom in a mental hospital so he doesn't have to deal with her. No word of her little brother yet," Clyde paused. "He's offering two hundred grand to anyone who gives information leading to Gracie's whereabouts. They've already had calls come in from drivers who had seen our van. It was caught on surveillance video at the Walgreen's. They've traced us as far as D.C."

Jessie took a moment to absorb the information. He never expected to be tracked as far north as D.C. That was too close for comfort. "They know we went north," Jessie thought out loud.

"But they don't know where we are, Boss. No one knows where we are except us," Clyde chimed in, hoping to keep Jessie from panicking again. Jessie had never been one to panic. In all the years they'd worked together, even if there were complications with a hit, Jessie never panicked. But since they took Gracie, panic was all Jessie could do.

Derek joined the conversation. "If someone had seen us farther north than D.C., they would have leads by now. They don't. It was snowing too heavily after D.C. for anyone to really be able to identify our van. And we threw off the other hit team when I got rid of the GPS. We're safe here."

Silence ensued for a few minutes until he heard the sound of dog feet on the floor above the kitchen. Gracie was up. He poured an extra cup of coffee and headed for the stairs.

* * *

She slept the best she had ever slept and wasn't ready to get up yet. But apparently two very large Bernese Mountain dogs had other plans for her. Brear and Honey proceeded to snuggle into the blankets in bed with her. She couldn't help but smile.

It had been a day and a half since she was abducted. All she did was sleep, but her body needed the rest. When she woke, she was famished. Her breathing was steadier, but her throat still burned.

Jessie walked into the room to find Gracie smiling and giving both dogs simultaneous belly rubs. He had seen her smile, but only from a distance. Seeing her smile up close, he thought she was even more beautiful than he had realized.

Gracie was very petite, yet strong for her size. Five feet two inches, only 110 pounds, her slenderness showed off her muscles. She loved to work out. Jessie often watched her from the parking lot of the gym she went to in the evenings. She had long auburn hair in natural spiral curls that reached her elbows. She was fair-skinned like her mother. She had light freckles covering the bridge of her nose and cheeks. And her ice blue eyes were stunning. Gracie assumed she had gotten her eyes from her father, but she would never know.

Her father died in a car accident before she was born. No more than a year later, when Gracie was only eight months old, her mother was married to Rudy Talbot. Her face was oval-shaped and she had high cheek bones with deep dimples. But her true beauty was her hair. Hardly anyone had seen hair like Gracie's. Her spiral curls looked like she had spent days on them, but they were completely natural. And her hair was thick, overwhelming for her petite figure. But that's what made it so much a part of her. When someone looked at Gracie, the first thing they saw was that hair, then those blue eyes and her smile with those dimples. Quite simply, she was a rare beauty.

In this situation, however, her hair was going to give her away and get her killed. She had to stay hidden. And that was Jessie's job.

"Good morning," he said as he walked over to her nightstand and set down a cup of coffee. "Thought you might like some."

"Thank you," she said quietly. She knew it made no difference, but she felt more comfortable with the dogs in bed with her. They were like a shield.

Jessie and Gracie were as awkward as a drunken one-night stand.

He sat on the edge of the bed thinking what to do next. She obviously liked the dogs, so he thought he'd start there.

"This big ol' thing here is Brear." Brear rolled over for another belly rub and groaned when he didn't get it. "And his partner in crime is Honey." They're my Bernese Mountain dogs, but it looks like they want to be yours."

Gracie was so confused. First they tried to kill her, then they tried to save her, then they were giving her their dogs? This was the weirdest bunch of killers she had ever met. Well, she had to admit, she had never met a group of killers, to her knowledge, so she really didn't have much to compare them to. Maybe they were all this sporadic.

"After that belly rub you gave them, I don't think they're going to be leaving your side." Jessie failed to tell her he had given the dogs a command to not leave her. They were highly trained guard dogs. But he had a feeling they wouldn't leave her anyway, even if he hadn't given them the command.

Gracie was waking up with help from the coffee Jessie gave her and she wanted answers. "I want to know everything," she said, her voice still raspy. She tried to clear her throat, but it did no good. "Is Rudy behind this?" She had a sneaking suspicion he was.

He sighed. Should he risk telling her the absolute truth? He had to. She'd find out anyway. "Rudy Talbot is part of one of the largest organized crime units in America. He married your mother for her money. Your father came from one of the wealthiest families in the country. His name was Michael Blanchen of Blanchen Hotels, the largest chain of upper-class hotels in this country and abroad. Your mother stood to inherit everything if your father died. One rainy night, his brakes stopped working. He hit a tree and died instantly. Rudy Talbot killed your father."

Gracie just stared at him. He couldn't gauge what she was thinking. Gracie knew absolutely nothing about her father. Her mother was never allowed to say anything about him, except that, occasionally when they were alone, she'd say Gracie looked just like him.

She had no idea she was the daughter of the owner of Blanchen Hotels. She had even stayed in them numerous times throughout her life. All she knew was that her father died before she was born. She never knew how.

"So if my mother inherited everything, wouldn't he be trying to kill her instead of me?" she asked, trying to piece together what her father's death had to do with her.

"No," Jessie said shaking his head, scooting a little closer to her on the bed. "If he kills your mother, you stand to inherit everything. Your mother had practically handed everything over to Rudy anyway, but if she died, it would all be taken out of his hands and put into yours. If you die, then he becomes the beneficiary."

She paused for a moment thinking that through. If that was the case then at least her mother and her brother would be safe. Her brother was Rudy's son. He'd want to have an heir to the fortune. But it still didn't make sense to her that Rudy would want her dead for money. "Rudy has his own money. He doesn't need my mother's. It's not going to make him any richer. That wouldn't be his primary motivation to kill me. And by the way, are you trying to kill me?"

Jessie knew Gracie was forthcoming, but he didn't know how much so. He chuckled at how easy she asked the question about her own fate.

"No! As I've told you, I'm not going to hurt you!" Jessie exclaimed.

Gracie silently stared into the fire. He'd already started telling her the truth, so he needed to finish. "My parents died when I was young. I needed to work for Rudy for the security he offered me, or I was going to be dead on the streets. My older cousins joined a gang. I would have followed right behind them. But I didn't want that life. Turning Rudy down wasn't really a choice. I've been working as a hit man for him for years. He's come to me three times asking me to kill you."

Jessie paused. She turned her head from the fire and stared at him, making eye contact for the first time. She held his gaze. He could tell she was trying to piece the puzzle together. "I threaten his chances for winning State Attorney General because I refuse to marry Phillip Proctor. And if Rudy can't get congratulatory votes... sympathy votes?" Gracie guessed.

"Could be," Jessie said. He hadn't thought of that himself. Gracie had good instincts. She would be a great asset to their team.

"That sick son of a bitch." She still held his gaze.

"Proctor wants you alive. Rudy wants you dead. We believe he had a second hit team following us. Someone attached a GPS to our van. Derek was smart enough to figure it out, and we threw them off our tracks in Jacksonville, although we've been traced as far north as D.C. No new news has come out, and nobody knows about my cabin, so we're safe here."

If Rudy wanted her dead for sympathy votes, why would he be pressuring her to marry Phillip? "I still don't understand why Rudy wants me dead. He and Phillip moved everything out of my apartment and into Phillip's. They practically have my entire wedding set up, and I overheard them talking of announcing an engagement right before the election. That would gain them votes too. So why does Rudy want me dead?"

Jessie shook his head. "He doesn't care if you're alive or dead. If you show up alive, you and Phillip get engaged before the election, and they gain congratulatory votes. If you die before the election, they both gain sympathy votes. But if he had a preference, he'd have you dead because you challenge him. You know too much, and you hate Phillip. Thing is, Phillip is stupid."

"No kidding," Gracie cut in.

"Phillip doesn't know Rudy wants you dead."

"Why didn't you kill me?"

Jessie took a breath and let it all out. "I fell in love with you the first time I saw you at that restaurant five years ago. I purposely botched the first three attempts on your life while we were planning how to rescue you from Rudy. When he came to me a fourth time, I knew if we didn't get you out of there, he was going to do it himself. So we staged an abduction, and tried to make it look like we killed you. But we had to rob a Walgreens pharmacy to get you your meds to keep you alive. The damn bastard knows you're not dead. I think he also knows my feelings for you and figured out I wasn't going to kill you. That's why there was a second hit crew. So now, Rudy's all over the media claiming you were abducted and is paying people for information."

Gracie was silent for a second. Then took a deep breath. "Bastard!" she yelled. "I knew he was capable of something like this. It was just a matter of time before I figured it out and he knew it."

Obviously Gracie knew more than she told. She might be a good accomplice on their mission to stay alive.

"We've met before?" Gracie half asked Jessie and half said to herself. She didn't remember meeting him.

"Yes. It was a small local outdoor restaurant in downtown Orlando," Jessie answered.

Gracie just nodded her head. She didn't remember him.

"Where's my mom and brother?"

He put his head down because he didn't want to see her reaction to his answer. "According to Rudy on the news reports, your mom had a breakdown and he put her in a mental hospital, which is actually a good thing!" He quickly added that last part as she started to interrupt him. She took two puffs from her inhaler. "He can't kill her in the hospital! And right now, she's safe. She's no good to him dead." Gracie had to agree with him.

"But Timmy, where's Timmy?" she asked in a panic. He might be Rudy's son, but he was also her brother. And Gracie and Timmy were unusually close. To get to her, all he had to do was go after Timmy and Rudy knew it. He could always have more sons. Timmy wasn't as safe as Jessie thought.

"There has never been any mention of Timmy. After your abduction, we haven't seen or heard anything about him through the media. But we know Rudy, and he's not going to do anything right now that will turn all eyes on him. We've got time to figure out what to do about Timmy."

Gracie sat up completely straight. "I want you to do the same thing to Timmy that you did to me. I'll even help. If Rudy knows I'm alive and wants to get to me, he'll go for Timmy. He knows that's the only true way to hurt me. I raised Timmy. He belongs with me!"

Jessie was afraid she was going to say that. Her request meant going back into the lion's den, and he wasn't willing to do that with her. But he knew she was right, and he wouldn't deny her anything she wanted. So they would have to find a way, eventually, to bring Timmy to her.

"Right now, we've gotta get you better and acclimated with the cabin and your new life. You can't ever go back, Gracie. It's not even an option. The only option you have is to stay here with us, with me. You'll always need protection as long as Rudy is alive." Jessie knew he put himself out there, but he didn't care. The truth was the truth and he always told it the way it was.

"I don't understand. Who is us?"

"There are five of us. We made up the hit team for Rudy. We're not bad guys. We just got a bad card handed to us in life. We did some pretty horrible things just to stay alive. We're good guys. We've got a couple of options, but it seems like the only one that keeps us all alive is to stay here, settle down, and make a life for ourselves. We're in the most remote location in the Pocono Mountains. It's a cute little town. No one will rat us out here. I think you'll like it. Small town, nice people."

She was quiet for a while. "So I'm living here now, in the mountains, with five hit men and two really big dogs."

He smiled and suppressed a laugh. He had wondered how she would see her new life. It was simpler than he could imagine. "Essentially."

"Do I get any say in this?"

"A little bit, but not much."

"Well what do I get a say in?"

Was he really willing to put himself all the way out there? Was he willing to face rejection so soon after he had her in his cabin? But he had to tell the truth.

"I've loved you since I first laid on eyes on you. Your choice is whether or not you want to spend your life with me. You have to spend it here, but you can choose if you want to spend it with me or not."

After he said it, he knew he couldn't take rejection, so he kept his head down and quickly left the room. Gracie sat in bed bewildered. She believed him. He had been nothing but nice to her and he saved her life. She knew Rudy was into some dirty business, but it surprised her just how deadly he was. Although deep down she did have a sneaking suspicion.

She felt protected by Jessie. Maybe it was the fact that he had risked his life to save her. Maybe it was that he had saved her life. He'd spent two nights giving her medication, keeping her warm, holding her in his arms. Maybe it was that she was brutally attracted to him and wanted to be with him. It slowly occurred to her as she sat in his bed that she really didn't have a choice. Her mind had already made itself up for her.

She managed to untangle herself from two hundred and thirty pounds of dog and made her way to the bathroom. Her clothes were neatly hung and dry. She put them in a pile and looked under the sink. There she found towels, soap, shampoo, conditioner, and even a razor. What she needed was a hot shower. Whenever Gracie needed to think through some serious business, she did so in a hot, steamy shower.

So her stepdad killed her father. Was she really that surprised? She had no extended family. If she did, she certainly didn't know about them. She knew her mother had money, but she didn't know how much. And Rudy had been glad to get rid of her when she turned eighteen, but also seemed to tighten the reigns on her at the same time. She didn't understand it, but she was sure it had something to do with her instincts regarding his profession. She knew it wasn't legal, whatever it was.

And then there was Jessie and the rest of his gang. They were killers too. But for different reasons. Rudy killed because he could. These guys killed because they had to. She doubted they killed the best citizens in the community. They seemed too gentle the night of the robbery, too caring to be that murderous.

So here she was, in the Pocono Mountains of all places. And this was where she was going to be. It made her sad, the thought of never seeing her mother or friends again. But her biggest fear was her little brother. They had to find a way to save him.

Chapter Six

Gracie got out of the shower and dried off. There was no blow dryer or make up. Just an old brush, but that would do for now. She was going to have to put together a list of things to get in town. Including warmer clothing. She put on her skirt, t-shirt, and tennis shoes. Then put the flannel over them. It was so long on her that it covered her skirt. It kept her arms warm, but her legs were freezing.

Composing herself, she decided to be brave and check out the rest of the cabin. After opening the bedroom door, the dogs ran out in front of her. So much for staying inconspicuous. She heard the voices downstairs go quiet and she wondered if she had made a mistake.

She decided to explore the upstairs first. Immediately to her right was a loft area, with a small room off the front of it. She thought it would be perfect for a nursery, or a room for Timmy. Funny, she never thought about babies before. She pushed the thought out of her mind.

To the left of her bedroom door, was a large walkway that spanned the length of the living room. At the end was a door to the second floor balcony, the same balcony the bedroom doors on either side of the fire place in the bedroom emptied out to.

Descending the stairs, she felt five sets of eyes on her. Looking over her shoulder halfway down the stairs, they all looked away, as if they had been caught doing something wrong. The only one who kept his eyes on her was Jessie.

At the bottom of the stairs she paused, unsure of what to do. The living room was massive. It had two oversized sofas and a love seat with numerous chairs around the exterior walls. The fire was in full blaze and everyone was in the kitchen and dinette area.

Jessie sensed her hesitation. "Gracie, why don't you come over here and get something to eat while I introduce you to the guys."

She was glad for the relief, and went straight to Jessie's side. He pulled out a bar stool at the kitchen counter top. She sat down, and the guys all gathered in the kitchen. Jessie stood behind her with a hand resting gently on the small of her back.

"I'm the cook around here," Clyde exclaimed. "That means I'm the only one who doesn't burn anything."

"I beg to differ. You killed last year's Christmas turkey. It was a crispy critter by the time you were done with it," Peter countered back.

"Man, you just don't know fine delicacy when it's handed to ya," Clyde retorted.

Gracie smiled. That's what they had hoped for: to make her feel at home.

"What can I make ya?" Clyde asked putting on an apron that looked more suited for an eighty-year-old grandma. It was covered in tiny pink and purple flowers with a white background. Not to mention the man was huge and he could barely fit the apron over his head. He looked absolutely ridiculous!

"Two eggs and toast. Sunny side up," she said with a little chuckle she was trying to suppress.

The whole time Clyde cooked, he and Peter bantered back and forth about who was cooking turkey for this Christmas, when Clyde should turn

Gracie's eggs, and how crispy the toast should be. Gracie couldn't help but notice these men sounded like brothers – the furthest thing from a massive killing operation.

After she was done eating, the house got quiet again. She looked at Clyde. "Thank you. That was delicious!" she said looking down. "I'm Gracie, but I'm guessing you all know that."

He gently took her hand and shook it. "I'm Clyde. I'm your new best friend!"

"Is that so?" she asked him. But that devilish look on his face made her know that he was absolutely right. She liked Clyde. The rest of the introductions were made before Gracie finally brought up the items she needed from town.

"You can't go into town," Jessie said. "But we can have some of the guys get you whatever you need. Just make a list."

She was disappointed. She wanted to see the new town she was going to be spending the rest of her life in.

"Can I ever go into town?" She asked.

He shook his head. "Eventually when things settle down. We have a computer set up in the basement. You can go down there and order whatever kind of clothes you need. Remember to get some really warm things. It stays cold up here most of the year. We really don't have a summer. Don't worry about the cost."

"What are you, a rich hit man?" she joked. She hadn't meant to let her brazen sense of humor out so quickly, but she had a problem with her internal filter. The filter didn't work.

Jessie chuckled. It was a sound Gracie realized she wanted to hear more of. "Something like that," he said.

She put together a list. Toiletries mostly. A

toothbrush, toothpaste, hair brush, ponytail holders, make-up, Advil for her headaches. By the time she was done her list was three pages long. She handed it to Jessie, who passed it off to Derek and Peter.

Derek looked at the three pages in shock. "Is this it? I don't think you have enough on here," he said sarcastically.

Jessie punched him in the arm. "Just go!" he said laughing. Gracie blushed. "Basement's the second door on your left, across from the bathroom," he said handing her his credit card. She took it and looked down the hallway. The action seemed too normal. Jessie, just handing over his credit card. That was something married couples did. Not people who just met each other. She hesitated.

"What's wrong?" he asked.

"Nothing," she lied.

"First, I'll give you the full tour of the house."

Jessie led her into each room, letting her know who was staying where. Finally he showed her the basement. It was freezing down there and Gracie was shivering. He took a blanket off the back of the couch and wrapped it around her. He pulled her closer to him. Every time she was that close, he didn't know if he could control himself enough not to kiss her. He put his arms around her and rubbed her back, trying to warm her up. She stood in front of him, her head inches away from his chest. The motion made her take a step forward and rest her cheek against his chest. His heart was beating quickly and she sighed with relief at the warmth. He was always so warm. Jessie knew if he didn't pull away, he'd kiss her, and he didn't want to scare her. He knew he loved her, but she needed time to adjust and figure out how she felt about him.

"Gracie, I'm not going to be able to control myself around you much longer. I've waited five years to have you with me." It was more of a warning than a statement.

He quickly turned away and walked upstairs. Gracie understood and for some reason, Jessie's openness regarding his feelings for her did not make her uncomfortable.

She settled in at the computer. Before she went on her online shopping spree, she Googled her name. A press conference from the night before appeared to be the latest piece of information. She clicked on it and turned up the volume.

Chief Burnell was surrounded by Rudy Talbot and the town's Catholic priest. "At this point, it appears as if Gracie Talbot's abductors are holding her hostage in order to collect a large sum of money from Mr. Talbot and try to force him to back down from the upcoming election. We haven't been able to track them past Washington, D.C. However, we do feel that Ms. Talbot's life is in great danger. She has a severe medical condition, and although supplies she needs were stolen from a pharmacy in Jacksonville, we don't know if she would have been able to stay alive long enough to receive those medications. There is a very good chance she is dead. However, we have not given up hope. This is still a search and rescue mission. These men are considered armed and highly dangerous. A tipster has led us to believe that at least fifty murders in Orlando and the surrounding areas may possibly be tied to them. We are still offering monetary rewards for any information that leads us to Gracie – dead or alive."

The press all started asking questions at once. "Where is Mrs. Talbot?" the loudest yelled.

"She is greatly devastated by this, and not able to handle the situation on her own. She will be in the mental health unit at the hospital until further notice."

Gracie noticed the smirk on Rudy's face and shook her head in anger. She was seeing red. As she went to turn the computer off, she heard the next question asked.

"Do you fear for the safety of your son, since it appears your daughter was abducted for your money and political reasons?"

Gracie froze. Her brother wasn't present at the press conference. At least he wasn't in view of the camera if he was. And there was something about the way the reporters were talking about politics. This wasn't about money. This was about votes. Her earlier prediction had been right. Rudy wanted sympathy votes. Phillip wanted congratulatory votes. But if that was the case, it still didn't make sense that Rudy wanted Gracie to marry Phillip.

"We have uncovered at least one plot to abduct Timothy Talbot during our investigation. Timothy is in a safe place where he cannot be harmed."

Was there really a plot to abduct Timmy, Gracie wondered? And if so, who was planning it? Jessie and his crew certainly weren't. And where was he? Was he at the house, or had they whisked him away somewhere? Her greatest fear was the thought that they weren't going to be able to find him. The fear struck her like lightning. She ran toward the stairs.

"Jessie!" she screamed.

He was in the basement in a matter of seconds. "What? What's wrong?"

She couldn't seem to get her words out fast enough. "There was a press conference. Yesterday. Mom's in the hospital, she'll be safe like you said," she rambled so quickly Jessie could hardly keep up with her. "But Timmy, they took him someplace. Or maybe he's still at the house, but they said he's somewhere out of danger. They said there's been a plot to abduct him so they took him to someplace safe. They lied! They know I'm alive! They know I want Timmy! They're going to use him to get to me!" Tears ran down her face and she was powerless to stop them. "I'm not going to be able to find him!"

Jessie wrapped his arms around her. "It's ok. I saw the press conference. Everything's going to be ok!"

"How can anything be ok? Rudy tried to have me killed! Now Timmy's missing! We have to find him. Rudy's going to have him killed too! He probably set up another fake abduction, or..."

Jessie cut her off. "We think Timmy's fine! We don't think there was a plot to abduct him. If there was, we would have known about it. We think he's got Timmy on lockdown in the house. We're not sure of it, but a cousin of mine saw cartoons playing through the window in his room." Jessie hadn't told her, but he was having his cousins in Orlando keep a close tab on the Talbot's property. They needed to know who all the key players were in this chess match and just watching the press conferences wasn't enough. Jessie didn't trust Rudy to not have a plan behind who showed their faces at the conferences and who didn't.

Gracie was furious. "How do you know you're the only people Rudy used? He's a sick and twisted man. You said yourself there was another hit team. He maintains his power in the community by playing people of the same regard off of each other. There's always more than one!" Gracie had an inside view of Rudy Talbot. It was something Jessie planned on tapping into, but he wasn't going to do it until he had her full trust and confidence, or she might not tell him everything she knew.

"He plays people off each other to get what he wants. He has a favorite, but right behind that favorite is someone to replace him immediately if

Rudy doesn't get his desired result. You said he tried to have me killed four times. And the fourth time you abducted me. If you botched it again, he'd have someone else do it. He would have another hit group that he would use. If you think you're the only hit team he uses to off people, you're wrong! And if you think that Rudy would tell you every plan he has, then you're wrong again. He may have told you about me, but he could have very well told the other guys about Timmy!"

Jessie knew if they messed up, Rudy would have them killed. But it never occurred to him that he had multiple hit crews until the night they took Gracie. What Gracie was saying made sense, but he was always in such close contact with Rudy, he never considered that Rudy would hide plans from him. Rudy had always been so forthcoming with all his intentions. Jessie didn't know how he would miss something like this.

"Now it all makes sense!" Jessie exclaimed. "Rudy already had another hit team! That's why he gave us up!"

Jessie and Gracie heard Derek and Peter come in through the front doors. They carried armloads of bags upstairs to Jessie's room. Jessie grabbed Gracie's hand, and they ran upstairs together. Jessie ran a hand through his hair.

"I made the mistake of thinking we were the only team," Jessie told his guys. "Rudy already had a second team in place to kill Gracie that night. Take the walkie-talkies and arm yourselves. Take inventory of the property. I want to know if one branch is out of place. I'll stay here with Gracie."

The guys opened up a kitchen cabinet and Gracie was shocked by the amount of guns and ammo inside. She wasn't used to seeing kitchen cabinets filled with ammunition. Within a minute, they were out the door.

Chapter Seven

"What are we going to do?" Gracie asked.

They sat at the dining room table, discussing their situation.

Jessie couldn't help but be protective. "We are doing nothing. You need clothes. You have to order some clothes, or you're going to freeze. Especially now. If we have to retreat into the woods, you'll die of hypothermia before we get there."

"No!" she yelled back. "I'm a part of this too. I need to do something! I can't just sit around here while Timmy's life is in danger. And Rudy is going to dangle Timmy's life in front of me until I cave and give myself away. That's what he did in the press conference, saying there was a hit out on him. There was no such thing, but he wants me to believe it."

Gracie was so upset her asthma starting acting up again. She was smart enough to put her inhaler in her pocket this time. She would never be caught without it again. She pulled it out and took two puffs.

Jessie gave her props. She had keen instincts. But he didn't anticipate her to be such a strong-willed woman. He could tell he was going to argue with more than talk to her. "Damn it, Gracie, you're going to have to trust me! You're not going to do anything. You're going to stay in this cabin, under the radar. Go downstairs and order clothes!"

"Like hell!" she said under her breath and pushed him backwards. She was stronger than she looked. She headed for the front door and grabbed the handle. But Jessie was quicker. His hand was over hers and he pulled her away from the door.

"Don't," he said in a deep voice that showed just how serious he was. It wasn't a demand. It was a threat.

"Or what?" she challenged. She was really going to make him mad over the years. He could see it now.

"You don't want to try me, Gracie," he warned. Jessie had a hell of a temper. He'd never hurt anyone with it, but he always got his way.

All the fear, all the anger, all the resentment of being put in this situation bubbled to the surface. She reached her hand back, faster than he saw it coming, and slapped him so hard across the left side of his face that his ears were ringing. It only occurred to her afterwards that she still did not know this man. And he could still be out to kill her. She turned and ran for the stairs.

It wasn't until she reached the top that she heard his footsteps on the first step. She could have sworn he took the steps five at a time. By the time she ran from the top of the stairs, which were directly in front of the bedroom door, into the room itself, he was right behind her. She was no more than two steps inside before he slammed the door shut, grabbed her right arm, swinging her around, pinning her between him and the door. She seemed to find herself in this situation a lot these days, she thought to herself.

She was so mad the terror left her body. They stared at each other for what seemed like eternity. She expected the worse. Instead, he leaned in and kissed her. Hard. She let out a noise from deep in her throat. Jessie thought he was going to lose all self control. She was pushing against his chest as hard as she could. He wasn't budging. But she realized she didn't want him to go away. She didn't want him to stop.

Gracie stopped shoving him away and grabbed two handfuls of his flannel shirt and pulled him closer to her. She kissed him back meeting her tongue with his. That was enough to make him lose all control. His kisses grew harder. He couldn't stop. And now she was kissing him back. Five years of wanting her, but not being able to have her, caught up with him.

He cupped her face with his hands, and then ran one hand around the back of her head to grab a handful of that thick, red, curly hair. He still had her pinned against the door and he could feel her heartbeat quicken against his chest.

In one rapid movement, Jessie jerked her skirt up around her waist. He picked her up. She wrapped her legs around his waist and hooked her feet together. He could feel the heat coming through her panties against his midsection. Lifting her shirt, he stepped back from the door for just a moment to pull it over her head. Then he unclasped her bra and took it off of her arms before he pinned her against the door again.

Gracie fumbled with Jessie's buttons on his shirt. She wasn't experienced at this kind of thing. She was only used to being propositioned by Phillip. But she wanted to feel Jessie's skin against hers. She wanted to feel that constant heat his skin provided.

Sliding his hand from the back of her neck, down her chest and cupping her breast, Gracie let out another low moan. Jessie bent his head to leave a trail of kisses up her neck, along her jawbone, until his lips met hers again.

Her kisses were becoming increasingly needy. She

needed him in a way she had never needed another man before. She wanted him and couldn't get enough of him.

Running his hands along Gracie's legs and gripping her butt, he lowered his hands to unbuckle his jeans and pull down the zipper. He pulled himself out, hard, throbbing, and ready to take her.

He stopped kissing her for just a moment and pulled his head back to look her in the eyes. "If you want me to stop, you're going to have to tell me right now, Gracie." It was another warning.

Gracie wasn't good with words. Especially in this situation, so she just wrapped her hands around the back of Jessie's head, lacing her fingers together in his wavy hair, and pulled his lips back to hers. That was answer enough for him.

In one swift movement, Jessie pulled aside Gracie's panties, and sat her down on his throbbing need for her. She sucked in a harsh breath and hugged Jessie to her as hard as she could. She wasn't prepared for the pain that came with his entrance.

Shit, he thought to himself. He had no idea this was Gracie's first time. But he had lost all self-control. Still pressed against the door, he slowly began to move in and out of her. She clung onto him for a few moments until the pain passed. Then she seemed to move along with him.

It didn't take him long to climax. Five years of waiting will ruin a man's romantic sensibility in the bedroom. He just took her with all the need that had built up inside of him. He had been rough. Too rough. He had hurt her. He promised her he never would. And now Jessie had already broken a promise.

Although Jessie emptied himself into her, he was nowhere near done with Gracie.

He quickly walked to the bed, and with all gentleness, laid her down. He pulled her skirt and panties down her legs, and threw them across the room. He wanted to feel every part of her, every curve she had. His hands roamed across her body, learning all her little secrets.

His hands felt wonderful and warm just like the rest of him. But they were rough, working man's hands. She loved the feel of them. She didn't want to admit it, but she had thought of Jessie in bed with her, doing more than just holding her tight as they slept the past few nights. How could she not when they were both half naked in bed together? He hadn't been inappropriate once. But she could tell that he had a lot of pent up emotions toward her, and now they were overflowing. She wanted to see how deep those emotions ran.

Meeting his demanding kiss, she finally finished unbuttoning his shirt, and let her hands roam widely along his chest and stomach. She wanted to feel the warmth of his skin and his racing heartbeat. As she moved her hands over his chest, he groaned with pleasure. She wasn't just accepting his advances, she was meeting them. She was an active player in their desire for each other.

He sent a trail of kisses across her cheek, under her chin, and down her throat. She let out a sound that he thought was going to kill him. He continued the trail of kisses until her nipple was inside his mouth. He teased her with his tongue and Gracie arched up to meet the warm, wet feeling on her sensitive nipple. Then he kissed the other one and Gracie felt like she was going jump out of her skin.

He stayed to the side of her, returning his lips to hers, letting his hands get to know every piece of her that was hidden by her clothing. And he wasn't going to stop until his hands had felt every part of her.

Finally, when it felt like he had teased her enough, she reached for him and said his name. His eyes locked with hers and he repositioned himself on top of her, and found his way inside her. She winced again at the initial pain, and Jessie cursed himself for not being more gentle. He tried to be as gentle as possible, but he knew she would be sore for the next few days. He never imagined this would have been Gracie's first time. He stopped and rested his forehead against hers. They were both breathing heavily.

"Are you ok?" he asked in his husky, deep voice that seemed even deeper with the emotion he was feeling.

She opened her eyes and locked her eyes with his. She couldn't say anything, so she just nodded her head, then repositioned herself, inviting him to take all he wanted of her. She held onto him, and locked her legs around him once again.

Gracie completely submitted to him, a move he didn't think the headstrong redhead could make. Neither one of them knew how long they had made love, but it felt like hours. Finally, when he had released all the passion he had been holding back for her, he let his body fall limp on top of her.

When he regained focus, regained his senses, he was still lying on her. He tenderly brushed a curl away from her face. She didn't know what to say. She didn't want him to move. She loved the heat he provided her. It was more than just body temperature. It was welcoming warmth that told her how much he cared about her. A sensual feeling that she knew only Jessie could give her.

Jessie lifted his head from her shoulder and kissed her ear, then her cheek, then her mouth. She lost herself in that kiss. It was a kiss that told her just how truthful he had been. Just how much he did love her, just how much he was going to protect her.

They both heard the guys downstairs, loudly cheering on a football game. It brought them both back to reality. Jessie didn't move.

"Did I hurt you?" he asked between kisses.

This time she found her voice. "No," she lied. He stopped kissing her and looked her in eyes. "Just a little, at first," she finally admitted. There was no lying to this man. He could see right through it. Her cheeks were red with embarrassment. She didn't want him to know she had never had sex before.

He kissed her, then rested his forehead against hers again. "Gracie, I didn't know."

She knew exactly what he was talking about. "Jessie, I wasn't saving myself for marriage. Just for love. Preferable for someone who would whisk me away on a white horse like in all the fairy tales I read growing up. But I guess a rusty old van will do." She let out a little laugh. To her, it was their story, their fairy tale. And that was enough.

He knew he hadn't forced her into it. Maybe he did force the kiss on her at first, but after that, he had no doubt about her reaction to him. She had wanted him as badly as he wanted her.

"If I had known it was your first time, I would have been so much more gentle. I would have made it the fairy tale of your dreams.

"Please don't apologize. It'll take all the romance away," she said in a whispering voice, afraid the guys downstairs might overhear something. That and she didn't trust her voice not to give out on her again. She was still under his spell and under his body.

He lifted his head to look at her face and smiled. "That was considered romantic?" He was amused. She had slapped the hell out of him, he chased her down and forced a kiss on her, which she eventually gave into, and she considered that romantic. She was going to challenge every notion he ever had about women.

"Don't tease!" she countered back. "And yes, that was romantic."

He just smiled. "My life just got a whole lot easier!" He was chuckling to himself. "Want to slap me again so we can go for round two?" Lying on top of her was making him want her again, and she could feel that ache for her beginning.

"Do I have a choice?" she asked.

"A little bit, but not much," he said again, reminiscent of an earlier conversation they had.

"What do I have a say in?" she asked, smiling. She liked the way he teased her, and she loved the way she felt when she was this close to him. She couldn't deny that she felt warm, protected, and loved. Her beating heart was completely safe with him, and at that moment, she willingly gave it to him.

"How do you want me to make love to you?" he asked.

"Every way possible," she answered. "Teach me everything."

Jessie smiled and let out a little laugh. "I won't teach you everything. That wouldn't leave any fun for later. But I will show you a few things."

He rolled on his back and grabbed Gracie, lifting her up and sitting her on top of him. "We'll start with this," Jessie said letting out a deep sigh as he positioned her on top of his ache for her. He kept her planted on top of him while he helped her move to their rhythm by keeping his hands firmly on her hips. Finally, when he thought he would go crazy, he rolled her over, repositioned himself on top of her again, and gently took her for the third time.

They made love until the early morning hours. When they managed to untangle themselves from each other, Jessie got up to start a new fire. They were too busy with each other to realize the old one had burnt out. Brear and Honey had jumped up and were cuddled together at the foot of the bed on Gracie's side. Since Gracie was still on Jessie's side, there was plenty of room for them on the king sized bed.

Jessie walked back around the bed, and crawled in, pulling the covers up around them to keep her warm. She snuggled into his chest. That's where she found her warmth. He kissed the top of her head, and she held him tight against her.

"I've been waiting five years for that," he said as Gracie yawned.

"That's a really long time," she said. "Why didn't you kidnap me sooner?"

"We had to try to pull it off like it was another hit. But I had never botched a single hit until you. After the third, Rudy knew something was up. When he came to us the fourth time, I knew I was out of time. I had to give you a chance at a new life. You deserved that." Gracie fell silent. When he looked down at her, he saw that she had fallen asleep. He kissed her forehead once more, and then nestled in under the covers and against her body for the rest of the night.

Chapter Eight

When Gracie awoke, Jessie was still sleeping. She couldn't believe this was happening to her. She had always dreamed of a knight in shining armor coming to rescue her from her third floor bedroom of the mansion she lived in growing up. But no one came until now. And the rescue wasn't exactly as she had pictured it, but it would make a great story for grandkids one day. And there she went again, thinking of kids. Why did she only do that since she began her stay in the cabin?

She had never thought of kids with Phillip. It was one of the reasons she detested him. Phillip hated children. Gracie loved them. He slept around with every wealthy girl in the community. She knew of at least two girls her age he had gotten pregnant and forced to have abortions. Phillip was too good to wear protection, or so he thought. Gracie despised him. She never let him kiss her, although he forced himself on her. She never let him hug her, even when he had her trapped in a corner. She told him she'd go to her grave before marrying him, and he just laughed in her face. She hated Phillip Proctor. She couldn't be more relieved that she no longer had to fear Phillip's increasingly inappropriate encounters toward her. She was going to spend the rest of her life right there, in the cabin with Jessie.

She didn't know what time it was, but the sun was

shining in through the French doors on either side of the fireplace. She looked at the hard lines on Jessie's face. She kissed his mouth gently. She didn't want to wake him, but she was hungry. Probably because she could smell the chicken in the air.

Jessie grunted and pulled her tighter toward him. She sighed and kissed the dimple on his chin, then his cheekbone, his eyebrow, and his mouth again. He stirred against her and she felt his need for her growing harder again.

"Keep that up," he said sleepily, "and you're going to get round four."

She smiled. "I'm hungry. But I'll take round four after we eat!" Gracie said. He noticed the change in the tone of her voice and opened his eyes, cocking his head back to see her face.

"You sound happy. Keep that up and you're going to give us away," he said. He hoped she was truly happy. It was his biggest fear: Gracie not being happy. Just pretending that she was, or just being outright miserable with him. But her tone suggested otherwise.

She blushed. "I am happy."

He gave her a quick kiss. Anything more would mean the beginning of round four and both of them were famished. He watched her get dressed and just smiled. Finally, he hopped out of bed and got dressed himself. He gave Gracie his thermal shirt and another flannel to wear instead of her t-shirt. There was another nor'easter blowing in and they could feel the draft coming through the doors. Even the fires in the cabin couldn't keep the chill out.

Jessie grabbed her hand and they started for the door. Gracie hesitated.

"Do they know?" she asked of the rest of the guys. She was one that also liked to keep her personal life private. But she had managed to hear the old bed sqeaking gently beneath them as they made love all night. She didn't know if that sound could be heard downstairs?

Jessie knew what she was talking about, but her shyness was adorable, and he couldn't help but play along.

"Know what?" he asked.

"You know, me and you."

"Probably. They know I've always wanted there to be a me and you." He paused a second, then sat down on the bottom edge of the bed. He pulled her so she was standing between his legs. They were eye level with each other. "You made love to me last night," she nodded her head in agreement. "Did you do it in the heat of the moment, or did you mean it? Did you want to make love to me?"

She could feel her checks on fire. She was blushing again. "I wouldn't have slept with you if I didn't. I wasn't saving myself for marriage; I was saving myself for the right guy. I guess I never got over all those childhood fairy tales. I finally got my prince who saved me."

"We don't sleep together, Gracie. We make love together. But is it really me you want, or the idea of what I did to you?" To Jessie, there was a very big difference. You sleep with people you don't care about. You make love to people you do. You love scenarios that save you and keep you alive. But that wasn't the same as loving someone.

Obviously this was important to him, to know that she really did want to make love to him. "Jessie, I really do want to make love to you. I didn't think it was possible to want someone so quickly. But I do," she finally answered.

She paused for a moment and shifted her weight between each leg. "I don't know what this feeling is. I've never had it before. But I know that I don't want it to end. I don't want to be without it. And you give it to me. So I don't want to be without you. I know it's only been a couple of days, but there's more to this than that. I may not have known it for the past five years, but I can see it now. It's you I wanted to make love to. It's you I was waiting to make love with for the first time. It's you, and even though I didn't know it until today, it's always been you."

Jessie smiled. He was a handsome creature when he smiled.

"But do they know?" Gracie asked again.

"Probably," he answered honestly. Jessie paused for a second. "Gracie, I've loved you since I saw you. You know that. I've done everything I could to protect you from that moment on. I'm sorry things came down to kidnapping you to keep you safe, but there's never been anyone else for me. My guys know that much. Their bedrooms are also underneath ours and my bed squeaks. So yah, they know."

"Ok!" she said completely embarrassed. "Then I guess they know!"

He chuckled. Jessie stood up and took her hand in his. They made their way downstairs. Clyde was cooking dinner and the guys were gathered around the kitchen countertop. Apparently they had made love all night long, and slept through the entire day. They couldn't help but notice Gracie in Jessie's clothes, and that they were holding hands. They also couldn't help but notice the red marks along Gracie's neck that Jessie left behind in his haste to have her.

When they got to the kitchen, Jessie sat down on the chair and pulled Gracie into his lap. No one said anything, but three of the four guys walked over and handed Clyde a thousand dollar bill.

Clyde looked a little sheepish, but he had the largest grin on his face. "Sorry, Boss! Over-under bet. I won!" he exclaimed. Apparently they had bet on how long it would take Jessie and Gracie to hit the sack. Clyde, knowing his main man, had bet less than one week. It had only taken two and a half days.

Bubba sat down next to them. "Surveillance of the premises is fine. We're all taking turns watching the shore and the gates. We found out our cell phone were tapped, but since we haven't used them, there's no problem there."

Jessie's eyebrows rose with suspicion. "So they were in our van too?" he asked.

"Yah," Derek confirmed.

"Has the rest of the van been checked out for microphones or anything of the sort?" Jessie demanded.

"Yes, and we didn't find anything. Still, we think that we should ditch the van someplace. I don't think it's wise to continue to use it," Derek added.

"Agreed," Jessie said. Usually he arranged all the small details, but the only detail he wanted to focus on was Gracie. He knew his guys could handle making decisions on their own, and if he was going to settle down with Gracie, he was going to have to let them make some. So he decided to give it a try. "Derek, why don't you work out all the details on that? But keep me up-to-date on everything."

The four other guys looked around in surprise. "Really?" Derek asked.

"Yah, you can do it. Run into any problems, let me know, but I have full confidence in you."

Derek was beaming. "Thanks, Boss!" he said. With that, he was out the door in a matter of seconds, heading to the garage where the van was parked.

"I can't believe I didn't see it sooner," Jessie pondered out loud. "We've never had one botched attempt at a homicide, except for Gracie. He knew how I felt after the first one. The second and third assaults were just testing me, if I'd changed my feelings any. This fourth attempt, if I didn't do it, those other guys would." Jessie was really beating himself up at the moment. There was no doubt that Gracie clouded his thoughts. When he thought about the past evening, he realized he hadn't even heard his guys come back in the house from surveillance. He was going to have to do something about that problem.

Jessie decided to delegate some more. "Clyde, I want you in charge of surveillance of the property. You keep track of who comes in and out, run all the property checks. But same as Derek, keep me up-to-date on everything, and let me know if you run into trouble."

Clyde gladly accepted the job, and immediately sent Peter and Bubba out to do another surveillance check before nightfall. The nor'easter was blowing in and the weather was getting nasty. He didn't want his guys out there at night.

"Boss," he said regaining Jessie's attention from his thoughts, "You've never delegated out jobs like this before." Clyde never missed a thing. And if something was amiss, he needed to know why.

"I want to settle down, Clyde," Jessie answered. Gracie, still sitting on Jessie's lap, just blushed and kept her face down toward the floor. "And it's long overdue. You guys can do this stuff. I need to let you."

Clyde knew where Jessie was coming from. He wanted time to be with his girl. He felt satisfied with that answer. And he knew Jessie wanted privacy. "I'm going to go check the perimeter of the house. We'll all be a couple of hours. You ok with that, Boss?"

Jessie was thankful to have a friend who could read him as steadily as Clyde could. "That's fine.

We'll be upstairs after we eat. Don't need to stay outside long. I'm worried about that damn nor'easter blowing in. Sky's looking dark already. Make sure all the guys are back in the house before nightfall."

Clyde left, and Jessie and Gracie helped themselves to a chicken dinner with stuffing and green beans. Clyde really was a good cook, she thought.

"How bad is the weather supposed to get?" Gracie asked a little nervous. She wasn't used to the North and the weather was unpredictable. Especially in the mountains.

"We'll probably get seven to ten feet. We'll be snowed in for a good while. Nothing to worry about though." Jessie tried to calm her nerves. He remembered his first winter in the cabin and the weather had him unnerved as well.

"I don't like the guys going out in it. Can't they just do security from the house?" Gracie liked the guys. And she was worried about them. It made Jessie smile.

"Yah," he said to make her feel better. "Tomorrow I'll make sure they do it from the house."

Trying not to be too obvious, Jessie decided to pry into Gracie's thoughts a little. "So you like the guys?"

She smiled. "Clyde's hilarious. He just cracks me up. I can also tell that he's closest to you out of everyone. Bubba is my big teddy bear. I always wanted a real live teddy bear. I like Derek's vocabulary. It seems to be made up of swear words. He's a boy after my own rebellious heart. And Peter. He doesn't say much, but he's perceptive."

Jessie was shocked Gracie took in so much in such a short amount of time. And she really hadn't spent much time around the rest of the guys yet. He had her in his room making love to her. She didn't have time to really get to know them. Yet she was right on the money with each of them.

"What about me?" he asked.

She sighed and sat back as she ate the last bite of food on her plate. "You," she said and thought for a moment. "You hold these guys together. They'd be lost without you. You are the heart of this family. They respect you, listen to you, and trust you with their lives. They love and respect you."

Jessie wasn't prepared for the picture Gracie painted of his relationship with his hit crew. He knew he was in charge, but he hadn't thought of himself as anything other than a big brother. He didn't feel he was worth the love and respect Gracie obviously saw the other guys held for him. Jessie was speechless.

He grabbed her hand, and took her right back upstairs.

Chapter Nine

Phillip viewed Gracie as a possession. And if he couldn't have her, no one could. Rudy knew that Jessie must have wanted to keep her for himself. Any man that looked at her wanted to keep her for himself. But Gracie, as Phillip saw it, was his territory. Rudy had promised him his stepdaughter in exchange for political support.

It infuriated Phillip that Rudy would keep knowledge from him that Conners had sexual intentions toward Gracie. Gracie was his! Phillip wanted to marry her, and he presumed Rudy wanted the same thing. Phillip had his own plans for Gracie and he didn't give a damn what Rudy thought about them. When Phillip learned about Jessie Conners, that's when he called his own men and made his own plan. No one was going to have Gracie Talbot if he couldn't.

Phillip was smart. He had his guys put the GPS tracker underneath the van where no one would find it. He had their cell phones tapped. He made sure that if this Conners guy was going to try to keep Gracie for himself, he'd be able to track him and kill him. Then, he would have Gracie to himself to do as he pleased. If she didn't cooperate, he would make her. But he hadn't planned on Conners' guys being so damn smart. They had found the GPS. And they hadn't used their cell phones. The police officer

Phillip befriended wasn't getting any more leads from the public. The trail went cold. For all he knew, Conners and Gracie could be out of the country by now. And every second he spent thinking about Gracie as Conners' property made his blood boil even hotter.

He had precisely planned the exact time when he and his men would take Gracie and have her begging him to release her into his possession. But Conners was as unpredictable as he was dangerous. He jumped the gun and now only questions remained. Where was Gracie and was she alive? How would they find her? If she was alive, how could they get her out of hiding?

Then it dawned on him. Rudy had mentioned after one of the press conferences that the only way to Gracie was through Timmy. Gracie loved Timmy with all her heart. They would dangle Timmy in front of Gracie like a carrot dangled in front of a horse. She'd have to come out of hiding if she was alive. He'd call Rudy first thing the next morning to set up an appointment to work out the logistics.

* * *

Gracie let Jessie lead her back upstairs. She stood close to the fire while Jessie started a new one. The winds were picking up and they could hear them howling against the doors. She was worried about the guys outside, but her fears were quickly calmed when she heard them come inside. She sat down to get closer to the fire. Brear and Honey had already claimed two spots, front and center of the fire.

Jessie rested on his side, propping himself up with one arm. Gracie, lay flat on her back, resting her head on Jessie's arm. He leisurely ran his hand through her hair, like it was the most natural thing for him to do.

"What was it like having Rudy for stepfather?" Jessie asked her. He needed to start getting inside her head, pulling out all the information only she knew.

"He was awful. He was mean and manipulative. Growing up, if there was one thing on the floor in your bedroom, he'd make you clean the entire mansion without the help of the staff. He always said he'd never be denied anything. Well I hated him every second of my life, so I tried to make him miserable. If he asked me for something, or to do something for him, I made sure I denied him of it. It was the dance we did for eighteen years. I never knew when I walked in the door if he was going to shoot me dead because he had enough of me." She paused, staring up at the ceiling. She was deep in thought.

"Did you know that he wanted me to marry Phillip Proctor, Senator Proctor's son?" she continued. "Rudy and the Senator are close confidants. They helped each other out, gave each other favors. They can't afford to not be each other's friends at this point. They depend on each other too much."

Jessie found that interesting. Rudy and the media were making such a big deal about the abduction having to do with Rudy's running for State Attorney General. "What do you mean, they're too close not to have anything to do with each other?"

"Well, public polls show a hatred for Phillip Proctor. However, everyone hates the other running mate for Senator, so it really comes down to what will win people over. Neither one is married. So if Phillip was married, he'd have the upper hand in the election. And since the Senator is a lame duck, Phillip can continue to run under a continuum of his issues. Add Rudy in there, and you've got a government set in its ways. To his credit, the Senator's done a pretty good job. And most people don't want to see too many changes right now. But Phillip isn't cut out for politics, and people know it. He's just riding on his father's coattails. He needs a wife. A steady wife to guide him. One who knows the ins and outs of public life. Someone like me."

"So you mean that Rudy and the senator were pressuring you to marry Phillip Proctor, the senator's son, so he'd win the election?"

She nodded her head and laughed. "I couldn't stand Phillip. He's been after me for the better part of five years. His advances were starting to scare me. They were increasingly inappropriate. The day you abducted me, he sexually assaulted me in my friend's apartment. He told me he was going to rape me that night if I didn't submit to him."

"What do you mean he sexually assaulted you?" Jessie asked, cupping her cheek with his hand.

"He cornered me against the wall, touched me at inappropriate places. Told me it was a warning for what I was going to get that night. He was mad because he and Rudy moved my things out of my apartment and put it in Phillip's. They did that just a few weeks ago. I've been staying with a friend. Had to buy all new clothes and everything. I wouldn't be caught dead in Phillip's apartment. I don't trust him behind closed doors. I've had close enough encounters with him to know better."

If Jessie understood her correctly, Rudy, the senator, and Phillip created an interesting little circle that was completely interdependent upon one another. Gracie was key to Phillip getting elected in place of his father. And Rudy needed Phillip and his electoral followers to get elected. But if Phillip didn't have Gracie, Rudy most likely wouldn't get elected, unless he got sympathy votes. But sympathy votes wouldn't help an unengaged Phillip and therefore wouldn't help Rudy because Rudy needed Phillip. It suddenly dawned on Jessie.

He abruptly sat up. "Gracie, don't you see it?"

Her head hit the floor, and Jessie didn't even notice it. He was onto something. "See what?" she asked sitting up, rubbing the back of her head.

"You're the key to their little circle."

She wrinkled her face. "To whose little circle? You've lost me."

"Senator's a lame duck right now. Phillip needs you to win the election. Rudy needs Phillip to win the election, so he can win. Sympathy votes will get Rudy in office, but not Phillip. Rudy knew I'd never kill you. But he needed a reason to get you to accept Phillip. You remember what you said about Rudy playing two people off each other?" Jessie watched her face for any reaction. But she just stared at him, absorbing the information.

"Yes. If Rudy told Phillip you wanted to kill me, Phillip would have taken me himself, though."

"Rudy only used me for hits. He had to disguise the real plan behind that. He doesn't really want you dead. He just wanted me to piss Phillip off enough for him to do something about you himself. And it seems like he did, and would have done more had I not have taken you. Rudy knew I wouldn't kill you. And he'd get more of a rise out of Phillip if he thought he had some competition."

"Phillip would want me, no matter what the price was on my behalf." Gracie added. "I'm just a piece of property to him."

Jessie smiled. "And he wouldn't want you to be my property."

Gracie smiled. "No, he wouldn't."

Jessie was starting to put it all together. "Did Phillip know about any of our hits?"

She thought for a second. "I think so."

"So then he'd know if Rudy contacted me, it would have been to kill you," Jessie concluded.

Gracie was starting to follow his thought process. "Oh my god! Phillip knew! He knew Rudy contracted you guys to kill me. And he would have known about the first three times."

"Rudy knew how I felt about you. I couldn't hide it, even from him," Jessie interrupted.

"He would have told Phillip, so Phillip could make some kind of move to take me. He wouldn't kill me. Rudy was trying to speed up the process between me and Phillip by telling him about you," Gracie added. "That's why he assaulted me that day. That's why he was going to rape me if I didn't agree to be with him that night! Rudy told him you were planning on taking me that night!"

Jessie swore. "There wasn't a second hit team. It was Phillip who was tracking us!" He shook his head. "How did I not see that?" The number of things Rudy had slipped past Jessie was really starting to piss him off.

"How would you know?" Gracie tried to console him.

"No, you don't understand. The day we took you, we could feel that something wasn't right. We knew Rudy would be staked out, watching us, which is why we staged the robbery. Really, we were just taking you, but we had to make it look like a robbery to the public. But we could feel something was wrong, so we moved in early. We beat Phillip to you that night. I always listen to my instincts and that night, they were telling me to move early." Jessie moved closer to her, as if just thinking about Phillip made him more protective of her.

"So let me get this straight. If you didn't take me that night, Phillip would have."

Jessie just nodded his head. "And Rudy was counting on me screwing up a fourth time. He never actually thought we would pull anything off."

"Did he ever hurt you?" Jessie asked, as protective as ever.

"He'd corner me if no one was looking and was more friendly with his hands than I would ever let him be. But he usually had a hand over my mouth, and he'd tell me that if I screamed, he'd hurt me or Timmy. Then he'd tell me that I only had limited time to deny him. He always sounded just like Rudy. It happened more than a few times. If I would speak up or fight back, I usually got backhanded. He backhanded me that day." She couldn't look at Jessie as she told him this.

Jessie was silent. He was going to murder that son of a bitch. Slowly. Very slowly.

Gracie looked up at him, and thought she could see the anger in Jessie's face. He grabbed the back of her head, and brought their lips together. He kissed her harder than he had the other night. His other hand wrapped around her back and he held her, kissing her as if his kiss could take all that Phillip had done to her away.

Slowly, he laid her down on the floor in front of the fireplace. He unbuttoned the flannel shirt she was wearing, then lifted off the thermal. He slid down her skirt and didn't stop undressing her until she was naked underneath him again. She shivered as a cold draft seeped in from underneath the French doors. Jessie pulled the comforter off of the bed and put it over her.

He stood over her, and started undressing himself. When their clothes made a pile on the floor, he repositioned himself over her.

"Are you still sore?"

"A little."

"Tell me if you want me to stop."

He found his way inside her. He waited for a moment to make sure Gracie was as comfortable as possible. If he had been a more patient man, he would have given her a few days to recover. But he wasn't and he couldn't hide it.

He made love to her again. Slow, gentle movements that made Gracie sigh.

When he emptied himself into her, he whispered, "You belong to me now."

"I know," she said when he buried his face in her hair and left the last pieces of himself inside her. "I don't want to belong to anybody else."

They lay on the floor in front of the fire, naked under the thick comforter Jessie had pulled off of the bed. Gracie fell asleep immediately. Jessie lay awake thinking of how fragile of a situation they were really in. Gracie was the key to the upcoming election and time was running out. Rudy, the senator, and Phillip would use every contact they had to figure out where Gracie was. And if they couldn't, they would drag her out using Timmy as bait. Jessie was confident that she was safe at the cabin, but he knew that Rudy and Phillip needed something major to happen before the election. And he had no doubt that they were in quite a predicament with elections only four months away. Rudy and Phillip would be hitting the campaign trail and they would be tapping every resource they had. Gracie's situation was worse than Jessie had originally thought. Rudy would just claim she was dead. But not Phillip. Phillip wouldn't stop until he found her.

Jessie finally fell asleep in the early morning hours thinking of ways to get to them before they got to Timmy and Gracie. Jessie realized they had to get to Rudy and Phillip before Phillip got to Gracie. He couldn't let that happen. But the only way to get to

Rudy and Phillip was to go back to Orlando and kill them.

Chapter Ten

"Why did you insist on waking me up at such an early hour?" Rudy spat at Phillip. The senator was busy with his duties today and it was just Rudy and Phillip in Rudy's office at the mansion. Phillip preferred it that way. What he had in mind wasn't for the weak-hearted.

"Because I know how to get to Gracie," Phillip said smugly.

Rudy's eyebrows shot up. "You found her?"

"Not yet. But I know how to."

"You stupid boy! Then why haven't you done it yet?" Rudy didn't have patience for games.

"Because I need to lure her out like a catfish waiting for a minnow to swim by his hole."

Rudy thought for a moment, then sat down in his chair behind his desk. "Keep talking."

"Gracie doesn't have many connections to Orlando. There really isn't anything keeping her here. Didn't you ever ask yourself why she didn't move away after she turned eighteen?" Phillip stopped for a moment, then continued when he realized Rudy wasn't going to answer. "Timmy," he simply said.

"What about him?" Rudy rudely asked.

"You said yourself he's the key to get Gracie to come out of hiding. If we stage a press conference saying that something has happened to Timmy, or that Timmy was hurt, Gracie will be here in a matter of minutes."

Rudy thought it over. It was true. Gracie was only staying in Orlando to be close to Timmy. And they were closer than he would have liked. Rudy didn't want Gracie having any relationship with Timmy. But he didn't have time for the boy and his wife certainly wasn't going to play mother. So Gracie was the best he got. And the more he thought about it, the more Rudy knew that Phillip was right.

"What do you have in mind regarding Timmy?"

Phillip smiled. "Keep him on lockdown in the house. We'll set up another press conference with breaking news tomorrow. It will be all over every front page of every newspaper in America. Timmy Talbot's abduction. Gracie won't be able to help herself. She'll be back here trying to take Timmy away by week's end. I guarantee it."

"Alright," Rudy said. "Let's do it. But if she's not back here by the end of the week, it's your ass on the line."

* * *

The next morning, Jessie headed downstairs while Gracie was in the shower. He told his guys what he and Gracie had uncovered the night before. Everyone was unnerved. They all agreed that they needed to get to Rudy and Phillip and kill them, before they could get to Gracie.

"Well, Boss, I think they're trying to get to her," Clyde said turning up the TV. Another press conference, with the title "Breaking News" running across the screen. "Apparently our boys want Gracie to think Timmy's been abducted."

"We knew they would do this," Jessie said. "I'll need to tell Gracie, but don't let her see this garbage!

It's just going to get her more upset. I have to get to Rudy and Phillip."

Clyde shook his head. "We must have a death wish! Rudy will never let us get that close to him now!"

"We're going to need more than five people," Jessie said

"How are we going to put this thing together? We're in the middle of the boondocks," Bubba added.

"I'll have to go away for awhile to get a group of guys together, but no one tell Gracie. I'm going back to Orlando and call on my cousins for help. I want both Phillip and Rudy dead. I want to be able to bring Timmy back here for Gracie."

"What are we supposed to tell Gracie?" Bubba asked.

He thought about leaving Gracie and his stomach dropped to the floor. He knew Bubba was more than capable of handling her and protecting her, but if he wasn't there, then it just wasn't good enough. And he wasn't ready to leave her. He hadn't had his fill of her yet. "I'll leave at the end of the week. Let's just let everything cool off a little bit. But I want around the clock surveillance of the entire property."

"When are ya gonna be back, Boss?" Bubba asked.

"As soon as I get my guys together. I'll either bring them back here or have you meet us," Jessie answered. "Right now, I need to tell Gracie about Timmy."

Gracie was still in her towel, trying to dry her hair with another when Jessie walked into the bathroom. The expression on his face spoke volumes.

"What is it?" Gracie asked.

"We knew they were going to do this Gracie, so try to not get too upset. It's all a part of their tactics to get to you," Jessie started.

"Timmy." She simply stated.

"Yeah. They're trying to get people to think someone abducted him."

Gracie gasped. "Well did they?"

Jessie just shook his head. Phillip and Rudy knew exactly what made Gracie weak at the knees. "I don't know one hundred percent, but Gracie, I'd bet my life it's just a tactic they're using to get to you."

She nodded trying to regain composure.

"What's the only thing you can think of doing right now?" he asked her.

"Going back to Florida to get Timmy," She answered without hesitation.

"Exactly."

Gracie sat down on the edge of the bathtub. "Goddamn it!" she yelled.

Jessie smiled. "You've been hanging around Derek too long."

Gracie let out a chuckle. She knew he was right. And she was expecting it all along. Like Jessie, she didn't really believe anything was wrong with Timmy. But they were trying everything they could to get to her. And she was determined to stand her ground and not let them.

* * *

The next few days seemed to fly by. Gracie had more fun playing in the snow with the dogs than she'd had in her entire life. Jessie just stood on the porch and watched her. She couldn't have been more excited about the jackets for the dogs that she ordered along with her winter wardrobe. Jessie argued that they were snow dogs and they didn't get cold, but Gracie knew how they snuggled in on her when Jessie wasn't in bed. She knew they got cold. Everyone laughed the first time she put the jackets on Brear and Honey. They looked so darn cute; she couldn't help but laugh too.

She had become one of them, asking about hits they took on the slimiest of scum in Orlando. It fascinated her how they dumped the bodies. She won every burping competition and laughed at this hilarious band of brothers. They taught her how to play poker, which they wished they hadn't because she won every round each night afterwards. Gracie failed to tell them, on purpose of course, she was incredibly gifted. Counting cards was one of her specialties.

The worst part of her days was watching the fake press conferences Rudy gave. But it gave Gracie a new purpose. She watched them with the guys, taking notes, jotting down everything that didn't make sense and that could be used against him. And with each conference, she desperately searched for Timmy. She was sure by this point Rudy had entered her mother into the mental hospital for good. But she'd tackle that later. Jessie was right about her being safe in there.

The best part of her days was Jessie. She loved going to sleep with him every night, while the fire burned to keep them warm. She loved him waking her up in the middle of the night to make love to her. Waking up to him in the morning was like a fairy tale come true.

One night, Gracie wondered into the room off the loft upstairs. There wasn't much in it. A desk with a chair and floor lamp. It had the most amazing bay window, just perfect for sitting and reading to a little baby. She walked over to it and sat down, her back to the door. It had the most majestic view of the mountains. All she could see were beautiful snow covered trees. She didn't hear Jessie follow her inside. He knew she didn't know he was there, lost in her own thoughts. Lately, he kept looking at this room and wondered what it would look like if they had a baby together. But he'd quickly thrown that idea away. A lot had to happen before that subject could come up. And he was going to be away for a while.

He made a little tapping noise at the door. Gracie startled and stood up, facing the doorway. "This room is adorable!" she said.

"Yah, I always thought so. Never knew what to use it for," he lied.

"It would make a great nursery for a baby," she blurted out before she could stop herself. She really needed to work on that internal filter. "Not that I was thinking anything like that..."

They both blushed. "No, I've often thought the same thing. Too bad a nice family doesn't live here."

"Yeah, exactly. Instead it gets stuck with us," she replied, relieved he gave her a way out of discussing that topic. "Anyway, the view is unbelievable. It looks like a painting from Thomas Kincaid or something."

Jessie walked into the room and stood behind her. "Yes it does," he said as he wrapped his arms around her and they stared at the beautiful wilderness all around them.

"Are you really happy here?" Jessie asked after awhile, breaking the silence.

"Surprisingly, I'm happier than I've ever been. After the past few weeks here, I can't imagine continuing my life back in Florida. The only thing missing is Timmy." How long have I been here?"

"Three weeks," Jessie said.

Gracie smiled thinking of the past three weeks and how they had taken shape. The first week it seemed like she was an outsider looking in. She took that week to recover from her almost deadly asthma attack. The second week, she felt accepted by this group of men, and by the third week, she felt like she had a new family. She couldn't imagine living without any of them.

They each had a charm she found irresistible. Bubba was the biggest guy she'd ever seen, but he cried like a baby at Hallmark commercials. Clyde was Jessie's conscience. They seemed to read each other's minds. Gracie had gotten used to looking to Clyde when she couldn't read Jessie. One always gave the other away. Derek was smart. He had street smarts that she marveled at. And then there was Peter. He was quiet and shy, but what he did say mattered and was important. No one knew the property better than he did. And while Clyde still managed the other guys when they did surveillance, he always sent Peter out first. He had a vivid memory and remembered exactly the way everything looked from the previous day.

And then there was Jessie. He was like the big brother everyone looked up to. He had street smarts and book smarts. He could figure people out. There was no lying to him. He could see right through you. He could be dark and he maintained a dangerous edge to him. But he was also loving, caring, and possessive. In contrast to Phillip, Jessie didn't see Gracie as his property. But she did belong to him, and she knew it. What surprised her even more was that she liked belonging to him. He made her feel wanted, loved, protected, safe, and warm. She couldn't imagine her days without him. She truly was happier than she had ever been.

Chapter Eleven

Friday night, one week later, Gracie stayed up late playing poker with everyone. She won, of course, and had all of them cursing like sailors while she walked away with four thousand dollars. Afterwards, they said they had a few things to work out, but Jessie promised he'd be up to kiss her goodnight.

When she got upstairs, she heard Jessie's low voice before she was able to close the door.

"Alright, everything's set. I leave tomorrow at daybreak. I don't know how long I'll be gone. Long enough to get my crew together and monitor the situation. I will not make a move until I can predict Rudy and Phillip's every move."

Gracie couldn't believe what she was hearing. Was he really planning on leaving her? She ran down the stairs.

"You're leaving?" she asked, breathless. "When the hell were you going to tell me?"

Damn, he thought! She wasn't supposed to know! "Gracie, please don't get upset."

She took two puffs from her inhaler. Her redheaded temper was spilling out and Jessie was going to receive the brunt of it.

"Let me explain...."

"No! I don't want you to explain! I want you to stay!"

"I can't stay. It's not safe. This is the safest thing

for you and Timmy."

She flew across the room and was standing on her tiptoes nose to nose with him. "Screw safety. That's all we've talked about since you took me! Let them take their shot. If it's my time, it's my time and there's nothing you can do to stop that!" Bubba, Clyde, Peter and Derek cleared the room like an atomic bomb went off. But neither Gracie nor Jessie noticed.

"Like hell! And just so you know, this plan...."

"I don't care what this plan involves," she cut in. "If it doesn't involve you staying, I don't want to know!" She felt tears welling up in her eyes, but she couldn't let Jessie see her cry. It was the only defense she had left against him, should she need one. And tonight, she did.

"Gracie, we have to get to them before they get to you. It's only a matter of time. You can't trust everyone, and this town knows we're here. Someone's bound to be swayed by the money Rudy's offering. It's a good town with good people, but there's always a bad egg. We have to plan on that happening. We can't be caught off guard. There are only five of us."

"So plan it from here. You don't have to go anywhere. You can't leave now anyway!" She was searching for anything that would make him stay, and suddenly it hit her like a ton of bricks.

He was losing his patience, but he tried to hold onto it, considering how upset he was at the thought of being away from her. And he had time to prepare himself to be away from her. Gracie hadn't had that time. "Four weeks, right?"

"What are you talking about?" Jessie was lost. Sometimes her mind went so fast, he couldn't follow her. She was too damn smart.

"How long have we been here?" she questioned him again.

"What does that have to do with anything?" He had no idea where she was going with this.

Her face turned red. Not from embarrassment, but from the realization. "Just answer the goddamn question," she yelled.

"Four weeks now." They were staring each other down.

"Figure it out," she said and walked away, leaving him completely clueless. She walked back up the stairs and wondered how long it would take him to figure out that she hadn't had a period since she got to the cabin. That, coupled with four solid weeks of unprotected sex. She was pregnant.

Jessie heard sniffles coming from the basement door. All four of the guys were poking their heads out. Slowly, they emerged from the safety of the basement. Gracie's fury was not something they wanted to be the brunt of. "What the hell are you crying about?" Jessie asked Bubba.

"That was just downright sad, Boss!" Bubba blew his nose in his handkerchief he kept in his back pocket.

"What the hell was she talking about? Why does it matter how long we've been here?" he asked more to himself than to his guys.

It was Derek that put two and two together immediately. "Boss, think about it."

"Jesus Christ!" he yelled. "I am! I can't figure out what the hell she's thinking!" He was desperate for an answer.

"Boss, she's pregnant. She's been here four weeks and hasn't asked any of us to go into town to get her whatever it is females use for that kind of thing. And the two of you aren't exactly quiet, so we know what's been going on," Derek said. It wasn't really a topic any of them were comfortable with.

Jessie's face went pale. Four weeks of unprotected

sex. What the hell did he expect?

"Boss, you don't look so good. You better sit down." Bubba said, finishing up wiping his nose. He looked at Clyde and whispered in an excited voice "I'm gonna be an uncle!" Clyde shot Bubba a look that could kill. But Bubba didn't seem to care.

"Oh my God," he let out under his breath as he sat down. He kept his eyes focused on the floor. He felt dizzy. He wasn't prepared for this. He didn't know how long he sat there, but he finally heard the shower start to run upstairs. It was enough to bring him out of his fog. By now, Jessie knew that Gracie took hot showers whenever she was upset and needed to think things through.

He stood up and walked upstairs more slowly than he ever had. He figured he'd better address the issue, or Gracie would be really pissed if he left without talking to her about it. But the thought of leaving pregnant Gracie had his stomach turning. He trusted his guys and knew she'd be fine with them. But when you added the baby to the mix, no one was good enough besides himself.

He walked into the bedroom, crossed the room to the bathroom door. He tried the knob and found it open. He knocked twice with his knuckles, then let himself in without waiting for her to say anything.

He leaned back against the countertop. "How long have you known?" he asked the shower curtain.

"It just came to me," she answered in a short tone of voice.

He shook his head. He still couldn't figure out how the hell her mind worked. "How far along are you?"

"I don't know. Probably a month."

He was tired of talking to the shower curtain. He pulled it back far enough to see her. She had just washed her hair. He turned the water off. She swung around and looked at him. He threw her a towel.

"Get out," he ordered. His patience had worn out.

She wrapped the towel around her and stepped onto the mat. Her hair was dripping wet.

"Why do I need to stay? Me leaving for a little while isn't gonna change anything. I'm coming back," he said.

"If you still think you need to go, knowing I'm pregnant with your baby, then go. You aren't the man I thought you were." She tried to walk out of the bathroom, but he grabbed her arm, hard.

"What the hell is that suppose to mean?" Now he was pissed. She had pushed his last button, and if he wasn't mistaken, he could have sworn she was trying to.

"Real men don't abandon their pregnant girlfriends." With that statement she not only pushed, but flicked the switch on his temper.

He took a step closer. His face had that dark and dangerous look Gracie knew not to mess with. But she was desperate. She had lost everything. She couldn't lose him as well. "Is that all you think you are? My girlfriend?"

She didn't answer him. She just stared him back in the eyes. She thought he'd be more upset by her comment than by calling herself his girlfriend. She tried to jerk her arm free, but he just tightened his grip.

"You know you're more than that to me." She expected him to yell at her, or turn and leave because she had pushed him so far. But she wasn't expecting the passionate kiss he gave her. He stopped just long enough to say "And I'd never abandon you, pregnant or not." He kissed her again.

She didn't know what to think. She had planned on him being angry with her. She had pushed every button she knew he had to get him to that point. Instead, he was being passionate and endearing.

"Don't go," she whispered when he stopped kissing her. He felt her shivering, standing there in just a towel dripping wet. "I can't lose you too."

That was all it took to do him in. He pulled her to him, and unwrapped the towel she had put around herself. He reached behind her and turned the shower back on. Jessie only stopped kissing her long enough to undress himself. Gracie just stared at him. He stepped into the steaming hot shower and pulled her back in with him.

They stood under the stream of water, their bodies hot and slick against each other. Jessie easily picked her up again and took a step to pin her against the warm shower tiles. He let her slip down just far enough to take all of him inside her.

"Jessie!" she exclaimed as he thrust inside her time and time again.

He took her with an angry passion. He was angry he had to leave her, especially pregnant. But he wouldn't leave without her knowing that she was more to him than his pregnant girlfriend. She was going to spend her life with him. And that only meant one thing to Jessie.

When he finished with her, he turned off the shower, and wrapped a fresh towel around her to dry her off. Once she was dry and in his flannel shirt for the night, he sat on the bed with her.

"Gracie, I told you that you belong to me now. And now you're carrying my baby. Do you really think you're just my girlfriend?" He couldn't believe she would think that.

"I don't know what else I should call myself. You haven't asked me to marry you, we're not engaged," she tried to get out the next sentence, but Jessie cut her off.

"Damn it, Gracie! Do I need to ask you? Marry me!" he yelled at her out of frustration. He got up from the side of the bed where he was sitting and paced the room, running a hand through his wet hair. "Marry me! I don't have a ring. I'm not good with words when it come to this. But I can't live without you. So marry me!"

Gracie didn't know what to say. She knew she would spend the rest of her life with Jessie. She didn't even have to think twice about that. But what they were to each other didn't really matter to her, as long as they were together. She didn't peg Jessie as the type who would want "husband" for a title. But apparently she was wrong.

"Jessie," she tried to say something but she couldn't get it out. All the words in her head seemed jumbled together.

"I'm not leaving to go be with someone else. I'm leaving to protect you and Timmy. I'm coming back. And now I'm gonna be a dad! Do you really think I would just want a casual relationship with you?"

"I didn't know what you were thinking," Gracie finally managed to say.

"What do you want, Gracie? You love the fairy tales. Am I supposed to get down on one knee? I don't have a ring, but I can get you one." He was desperate for her answer.

"No," she said. "No, I don't want you to get down on one knee. I don't need a ring. And yes, I will marry you!" she said as he crossed the room to her and forcefully kissed her, making her fall back onto the bed.

When he lifted his head, he was smiling. So was she. And a little laugh escaped her throat. He had all but tackled her in bed.

"You're going to be my wife," he said.

"And the mother of your child," she added.

"I'm not leaving you Gracie. I'm coming back. With Timmy."

She nodded. "I still don't want you to go. I don't know how to be without you anymore." She really didn't. Her whole world had begun to revolve around Jessie.

"I'll be back," he told her as he held her in his arms.

He gently rubbed her back to help her fall asleep. She cried herself to sleep in his arms, and he was careful not to wake her when he pulled his arm out from underneath her.

It was the middle of the night before he made it back downstairs. The guys were dispersed throughout the living room waiting for him.

"Let's get this finished." Jessie sat down at the table with the guys, and they went over everything. From the cars they would use to the cell phones to communicate. What to do if Phillip found them. How to teach Gracie to stay safe in the cabin if an ambush did happen. Every detail was discussed until it was three am. Jessie only had about four hours left until he had to leave. And the reality that he was about to go after one of the most powerful men in American organized crime was starting to weigh down on him. There was an underlying understanding among his guys that he might not make it back.

Bubba stopped him at the bottom of the stairs while the other guys retired to their rooms for the night. "Hey, Boss," he was talking under his breath so no one else would hear. "If you don't come back..." he trailed off.

"Just keep her happy. Give her whatever she wants. Keep her remote and keep her safe." He turned to walk up the stairs, but stopped and turned back around. "And make sure she and the baby know just how much I love them." With that, he turned to climb the stairs.

When he got upstairs, the fire was burning low. He put on a few more logs, then sat at the edge of the bed and stared at her. She was perfect. Absolutely beautiful in every way possible.

She stirred in her sleep when he crawled into bed and slowly opened her eyes. She already had tears welling up again, and they poured out within seconds. "Don't go," she pleaded.

"I have to."

"No you don't. Just stay here with me and the baby!"

He hugged her to him. She was fragile tonight; he could see it in her face. She was pale, and just didn't look quite right. He chalked it up to her being upset over him leaving. She clung to him and wouldn't let him go. They both fell asleep still intertwined, connected.

* * *

Clyde woke him and then left the room so Jessie could dress and begin his mission. When he climbed out of bed, he ordered the dogs to take his place. They did so with the utmost care not to wake her. He didn't dare wake her now. He got ready with deliberate slowness. He just couldn't take his eyes off of her. Before he walked out the door, he stared hard at Gracie for a few minutes. Maybe it was his imagination, but he could have sworn he saw a little baby bump bulging out from her stomach under the covers. He put his hand on it, and then bent down and gently kissed the baby.

Walking into the small bedroom off the loft, the one perfect for a baby, he grabbed a piece of paper on the desk.

"I'm going to come back," he wrote. "In the meantime, listen to the guys. They know what's going on. I need you to know everything they are going to teach you before I get back. I love you. Please take care of yourself and the baby."

He went back into the bedroom. He kissed the top of her forehead, her cheek, and then her lips, before turning around and leaving the room.

He said his goodbyes to his crew and asked Bubba to walk outside with him. "I want you to keep an especially close eye on Gracie. Sleep upstairs in the loft, so she doesn't feel alone. Teach her everything I told you. I need her to know it for when I get back. Remember what we talked about last night. Always stay with her, keep her safe, and make her happy. And stop crying!"

Bubba just couldn't help it. He was a softy. "Sorry, Boss! I'll do everything you asked!" Jessie knew he would.

He walked to the unattached garage at the bottom of the property with Bubba. Together, they carried two large duffle bags. One filled with personal belongings, extra passports, different currencies, a number of different alias driver licenses, birth certificates, and social security cards. The other filled with protection: guns, grenades, ammunition, and any other toy that might be of use to them.

They loaded each bag with care into the back of the Tahoe. Jessie wasn't worried about the guns being at the back of the truck. He wore a gun harness and had one strapped to his ankle. He was covered and ready to kill.

* * *

Gracie rose late in the morning. She didn't know what time it was when she woke up. Looking at the clock, she saw it was eleven thirty. Panic struck her as she looked to her left and saw that the dogs had taken the place of Jessie. She ran downstairs, unaware that she was just wearing Jessie's flannel shirt. Bubba was sitting in the living room waiting for her. Everyone else was out inspecting the property. He was expecting her and stood up when she walked into the room.

"Is he gone?" she asked him.

Bubba's eyes filled up with tears. "Yes ma'am," he said with his head down.

She just stood there. Could he really be gone? Did he really leave without saying goodbye? Apparently he had. At first she was shocked. She took two puffs of her inhaler. Then that shock hit her like a punch to her stomach.

Bubba followed her up the stairs but kept a close distance behind her. He was prepared for her to scream and yell, to hit him and cry. He was not prepared for her to get sick in the bathroom.

"He's not gone for good," Bubba half-lied sitting on the edge of the bed.

She came out of the bathroom looking pale, with one hand on her stomach, and the other across her mouth.

"Jessie's gone." Her eyes welled up with tears again, but this time she shoved them back down. She sat on the edge of the bed, facing the door. "He asked me to marry him last night."

Time stood still and Gracie felt her breath leave her body, but she couldn't breathe anything back in.

"Gracie ma'am, you alright? It's going to be ok," Bubba said, putting an arm around her back, hugging her to him. He was like a big ol' grizzly bear that you just wanted to wrap your arms around. She hugged him back and tried to regain her breathing. But her heart was pounding. Sweat was beading up on her forehead. Her ears were ringing and black and white spots clouded her vision. She was in a full blown panic attack. She reached into her pocket and took another two puffs of her inhaler as she tried to calm down.

Chapter Twelve

Jessie drove for sixteen hours, only stopping twice. He felt fairly certain that he would be safe nestled in the historic district of St. Augustine, Florida. The bed and breakfasts had rear parking with minimal lighting. It was the perfect place for him to set up his headquarters as he staged this hit. He also knew that St. Augustine was a vacation destination for a lot of Rudy's "employees" but none of them lived in the area. It was the first week of December, and St. Augustine was only reaching a high of fifty degrees, so there weren't many tourists.

He chose the Inn on Charlotte because it was one block from the inlet and one block from Ponce de Leon Boulevard. It was also poorly lit and they had a vacancy in their suite.

After being shown to his room on the first floor, Jessie unloaded his two duffle bags, and began to organize the room as he saw fit to protect himself. He radioed the guys to let them know he had reached his destination. After unpacking, he settled in for the night and fell asleep with thoughts of Gracie on his mind.

The next morning, Jessie had coffee and breakfast with a couple that was staying at the B & B. They were from Michigan, celebrating their thirtieth wedding anniversary. Besides the Inn Keeper, they were the only people who had seen Jessie.

"Congratulations," he told the couple who were beaming with happiness.

"Are you married, son?" the older gentleman asked.

Jessie smiled. "Engaged with a little one on the way."

"Oh how dear!" the wife exclaimed. "Are they here?"

"No," Jessie sighed. "I'm only here on business."

"Well what a shame! It's so beautiful!" she said.

Jessie smiled. "Maybe I'll bring her here for our thirtieth wedding anniversary! It is a very romantic place."

After a few more minutes of casual conversation with the couple, Jessie broke away to go back to his suite. He sat down at his desk and listed the names of the guys he was going to call.

The last time Jessie was "finding" guys to work with, he and Clyde just seemed to fall into acquaintance with the other four. And they had just clicked. This time, Jessie wasn't taking chances. He knew whom to call.

Jessie had some older cousins that formed their own gang in Orlando. He had stayed in close contact with them through the years. They weren't big hitters, they just had their territory and didn't let anyone else into it. They knew Jessie was in the larger circle of the organized crime network, but they didn't know how deep. Jessie knew they weren't experienced hit men, but he did know that they had killed before. But loyalty, he could guarantee. And that's what he needed. Guys willing to lay down their life for you and yours.

The phone rang several times before Landon answered the phone. "Hello."

"Landon, it's Jessie."

"What's going on? I've been seeing pictures of your

face all over TV. Seems you got yourself into a hot mess," Landon said, laughing into the phone at the other end. "Is she worth it?"

"Absolutely," Jessie responded with a smile. And that TV picture was the reason why he was growing a beard now, itchy as it was. "Listen, I need you, Luka and Gavin. It's serious."

"Tell me when and where." That's what Jessie was counting on. Family ties. Landon was the oldest cousin. His little brother Luka was the youngest cousin. Gavin was another cousin the same age as Jessie. After this, Jessie fully intended on bringing them into their group in the mountains. The three men were perfect for this. Unattached, they brought no baggage or families along with them. Just themselves and their lethal abilities.

Jessie gave him the basics, and told him to meet him on a chartered boat tomorrow morning at eight am. Then he hung up the phone. Not able to get Gracie off his mind, he radioed in again and asked specifically for Bubba. Bubba was hesitant and had insisted that Gracie was sleeping when he asked for her. Originally, Jessie didn't want Gracie to know that they could radio back and forth, but he changed his mind. Bubba wasn't sure yet that Gracie should know.

There was nothing more he could do that day, so he went to bed early, prepared to start plotting the death of Rudy Talbot the very next day.

* * *

Landon and Luka arrived at the docks first, followed by Gavin a few minutes later. They all exchanged hugs, not having seen each other in months. They were, by all accounts, a menacing looking crew. Each above six foot tall, heavily muscular, hard lines on their faces from years on the street. They drew attention to themselves and they knew it. They would have to meet at inconspicuous places to not be noticed.

Once out to sea, Jessie told them everything from the first time he saw Gracie, to the three botched attempts on her life, the abduction, and everything he knew about Rudy Talbot and Phillip Proctor. The cousins weren't in the dark about Rudy. Everyone in Orlando operated around Rudy Talbot. No one stepped on his toes, or you met up with the likes of Jessie. But by being blood relatives, Landon, Luka, and Gavin got away with a lot more. Helping Jessie now was a sort of "repayment" for all those years.

"I don't know how we're going to pull this off," Landon said. "He's always got his people around him. And if you're spotted once, you're as good as dead! Not only that, but Phillip's been poking around our territory. He's had a couple of guys try to threaten us into giving them information about you."

Jessie just shook his head. He wasn't surprised they were going after his kin. "What did you tell them?"

The three just laughed. "We didn't tell them anything. I just pulled my gun out and started shooting at his feet. He got off my lawn faster than Happy Feet."

Jessie laughed too. That sounded exactly like something Landon would do. His gun always spoke louder words than he did.

"There are a few other matters we need to take into consideration." Jessie continued with the story of Timmy. Jessie wasn't certain Timmy was at the house.

Finally, he told them the biggest news. "My biggest concern is Gracie. She's pregnant."

Shock and silence filled the air. No one knew what

to say. But Landon broke the silence first. "So you really are in love with her aren't you?"

Jessie just looked out to sea. There were no words for how much he loved her and how he felt about her. "I've asked her to marry me. She said yes."

Gavin was excellent about coming up with plans. Jessie didn't know why he wasn't already a part of his group. And talking of Gracie made his mind start whirling with ideas.

"What we need to do is get inside his newest posse. Not necessarily the big wigs, but the mansion staff. The staff members always have a better idea of what's going on, people's behaviors; you know what I'm talking about. And, the inner staff will have everything we need to know about Timmy."

Gavin was silent while everyone looked at him. He was right and they all knew it. But he had that look on his face like he wasn't done thinking yet. And he was not. "We need to abduct Timmy first before we kill Rudy. We can't chance Phillip or Rudy harming Timmy to get to Gracie. They both know that the surest way to get Gracie to come out of hiding is to go after Timmy. If they take him somewhere, they know Gracie will start to look for him. If they hurt him, they know Gracie will come back for revenge. They are dangling him in front of her right now to see what she is going to do. And I wouldn't put it past them to hurt Timmy just to get back at her if she does nothing. So there is a great need to get to Timmy as soon as we can."

Jessie agreed. For the next few hours, the four contemplated how they could go about getting to the staff. One person kept coming back to mind. Gracie. She could be the key to unlock this whole mess. If they could get Gracie back to Orlando, and get her to convince her former staff members they were safe with her, Jessie and his crew could get inside Rudy's home. Closer than they ever thought possible. But Jessie didn't like the thought of Gracie being so close to someone who wanted her dead.

"Think about it Jessie," Luka pleaded. "The last thing they are going to do is expect her to go back to the house. She's safer inside the lion's den. She's navigated it for twenty-six years. She's safer there for a few minutes than she is in your mountain hideaway."

Jessie had to agree. Right now, Gracie was a sitting duck. She had to come back to Florida. She had to get into the servants' quarters and set the plan in motion. She was the key to her own survival. But first, a few things had to be ironed out.

Which servants could Gracie trust with her life and Timmy's? How was Timmy's new life without Gracie, and when could she whisk him away? Where would they stay? How could they get inside the house to kill Rudy, and then escape while placing the blame elsewhere? Jessie liked to think they could frame Rudy's death around Phillip Proctor. Gracie was thought to be dead, Phillip still wanted what had been promised to him, and so he murdered Rudy Talbot. They could pull it off. But the details had to be perfect. And Jessie had to put the woman he loved in danger.

When the men got back to shore, they each headed in their own directions. The other three cousins were staying in various B & B's around the historic district so they could be in close contact, yet wouldn't be seen together.

Jessie spent Christmas and New Years plotting with his cousins and putting together a plan so that when Gracie arrived in St. Augustine, they would be ready to go. It was hard to plan the execution of everything. Both Phillip and Rudy had already taken to the campaign trail. Jessie and his cousins spent

January and half of February on constant
surveillance of Phillip and Rudy. They followed them
during their travels, making sure they didn't get
anywhere near the Poconos hideaway. With all their
traveling, it was difficult to pin down when they
would be home.

By February, they had a good idea of what needed
to happen and when. The guys knew that Phillip and
Rudy would be home the last week of February
campaigning in their own city of Orlando. Now he
just needed Gracie.

* * *

Three months had gone by since Gracie had seen
Jessie. She followed Jessie's directions, and learned
everything she needed to know about staying alive.
They taught her how to fire a gun, stay covered in
the trees, how their hits worked, and what her part
in them would be. She was determined to not let
them down. She wanted to be an integral part of her
new family. She truly believed that when it was her
time to go, it was her time. That ideology led to some
fearless training that the guys were impressed with.
She was a natural. Yet as the months went on, her
growing stomach was becoming a concern.

It was the end of February and one of the coldest
nights of the year. Sitting around the dinner table,
they were all laughing as they watched Brear and
Honey through the kitchen windows, sporting their
winter coats, frolicking outside in the snow. Jessie
never radioed in until the early morning hours, but
his voice came across the radio in the kitchen loud
and clear at dinner time.

"Base 1 to camp, Base 1 to camp." It was
undeniably Jessie's voice. And Gracie froze. Bubba
grabbed her hand, like he had become accustomed

to do when she felt afraid, scared, or just didn't know what to do.

Clyde jumped up out of his chair. "This is camp. Everything alright at Base 1?"

"Everything's fine. We've got a plan set to go in motion. We need you guys to pack up and head south to Base 1." Everyone looked at each other in confusion.

"Are you sure about that, Boss?" Clyde asked.

"I need you to move first thing in the morning. Pack tonight and leave early. I need you to be here by tomorrow night so we can begin briefing you the following day." Jessie's voice was tense and everyone could feel it.

"Who all is we?" Clyde asked.

"That includes Gracie," he said after a few seconds of hesitation. "I need Gracie to pull this operation off."

Gracie didn't want to leave. This cabin had become her home, her safe haven. But she wanted to see Jessie.

"Let me talk to her privately," he said.

Clyde handed Gracie the radio and then left the room with the other guys.

"Jessie," she said quietly.

"Hey you," he said with relief in his voice. He terribly missed the sound of her voice. "Are you ok?"

"Yeah. I've been doing everything you asked. I know everything I need to know," she said quickly. She wanted Jessie to know she hadn't let him down.

"The baby..." he said, trailing off. He still wasn't sure how to bring up the subject or ask about it.

She let out a sigh as she smiled. "Growing quickly," she said putting a hand on her large stomach. "I'm so big I have a feeling it's a boy, and he's going to be a big one like his daddy."

Jessie smiled, but didn't respond. He closed his

eyes to try to imagine what Gracie looked like with a pregnant belly.

"You're coming to me," he finally said. "I'll see you tomorrow night."

"Will we be coming back here?" she asked.

"I hope so," Jessie answered not wanting to give false hope.

Gracie smiled and a tear left her eye. "I've missed you," she whispered into the receiver.

"I've missed you more. Rest up and take care of the baby. I'll see you tomorrow." They hung up the receivers, and Gracie made her way upstairs to pack.

She finished packing all her things, and then she settled in for her last night in the cabin. Bubba promised the dogs would be well taken care of when she was away. Somehow, that made her feel better.

She awoke at five am to Bubba gently knocking on the door. She was ready to go in thirty minutes. She said her tearful goodbye to each room in the house and to the dogs. Then they were off, back on their way down to Florida.

Driving down to Florida in another black Tahoe, she noticed the seats were much more comfortable than sitting on a van floor. But they had to stop often. She was carrying the baby low, and it felt like he was putting all his weight on her bladder. She stopped counting the number of bathroom breaks she had to take around ten. She had finally fallen asleep with her head on Bubba's leg around nine pm.

They arrived in St. Augustine at the Inn on Charlotte around one am, under the cover of darkness. Clyde radioed to Jessie, who stepped out of a back door only a few seconds later. Clyde hopped out and gave him a bear hug. Jessie had reserved the rest of the rooms at the inn for his guys. Gracie was to stay in his room.

Derek, Peter, and Clyde all climbed out of the

SUV.

"Where's Gracie?" Jessie asked with anticipation.

"She's sleeping on Bubba," Derek informed him.

Bubba slowly shook her shoulder. "Gracie, we're here," he said quietly. She slowly opened her eyes, yawned, and stretched.

"We're in St. Augustine?" she asked sitting up. It was her favorite place to visit. She went there frequently growing up to get away from the daily horrors of living with Rudy.

"Yah, we're here. Jessie just took the guys inside to show them their rooms. We need to go inside now."

They got out of the car and entered the back door to Jessie's room. Bubba put her suitcases down, secured the back door, and then left to find the rest of the guys.

She heard him come in the room before she saw him. The door closed behind him and she heard him whisper "Gracie" under his breath. She turned to face him and blushed as he settled his eyes on her baby bump. But she was too overjoyed to see him. She rushed to him and wrapped her arms around his neck, pressing her face hard into the crevasse of his neck and shoulder. His hair had gotten longer, and he had a beard, but he was her Jessie.

"Jessie...," she said hugging him tightly to her. He could feel her stomach between them and was amazed at how natural it felt. They held onto each other for what felt like eternity. Finally, when the realization set in that she was no longer without him, she loosened her grip and lifted her face to look at him.

Jessie took her by her hand and led her to the bed, sitting down with her. She kicked off her shoes, and yawned. He put a hand on her stomach and felt the baby kick him. It startled him, and he yanked his hand away. Gracie smiled. She reached for his hand and then put it back on her stomach. "He's an active little guy."

"What makes you so sure it's a boy?" Jessie asked.

"I don't know. It's a big baby. But I just have this feeling," she said leaning back on her arms.

They took in the moment. Jessie couldn't take his eyes off her. She couldn't stop watching him watch her.

"Please don't ever leave me again!" she half whispered, half pleaded.

He looked up at her, and laid her down gently on the bed. "I promise," he said.

He knew she was tired, but he had been apart from her for three months. He wasn't going to go another night without making love to her. He went to unbutton her jeans and found that she was wearing them unbuttoned to begin with. He dropped them next to the bed. He carefully took off the rest of her clothes so she lay naked on top of the covers. And he just took in the sight of her. She was even more beautiful than he remembered. And even more beautiful pregnant.

Her skin was stretched and he could see the veins underneath. Her belly button had popped out, but what really captivated him was the way he could see her stomach moving around when the baby moved.

He climbed into bed with her, kissing her. It was a kiss that exposed the heartache each of them had experienced being away from each other. It was a kiss of promises for the future. No time away could change the growing feelings they had for each other. The absence had made both their loving hearts grow fonder.

He kissed every inch of her skin. She missed the way his kisses felt, so soft and warm from such a hard and dangerous man. And the kisses on her stomach were so sensual. With her skin stretched thin, his warm lips made the baby active. With one kiss, the baby kicked Jessie right in the mouth. Both he and Gracie laughed.

Gracie's stomach was big, but if Jessie kept his arms straight on either side of her, he was able to not put any pressure on her stomach. He took off his clothes and climbed on top of her, making sure not to put any pressure on the baby. Gracie reached up and laced her fingers with Jessie's on either side of her head. She held onto him as he made up for lost time.

When they finished with each other, he pulled her close and wrapped the blankets around her. She rested her head on his shoulder, with an arm and a leg sprawled across him. Her stomach also rested against him.

"I never got a chance to tell you in the mountains," she said as her eyes slowly drifted off to sleep, "that I love you."

Chapter Thirteen

The guys awoke in the morning and all gathered in the main room to have breakfast. Gracie was sound asleep and Jessie wasn't going to disturb her. They had made love until the early morning hours. She'd need her sleep. Landon, Luka, and Gavin arrived after a little while. Everyone said their hellos and they summoned in the owner of the B & B.

Claudia was a middle-aged woman who kept to herself. She knew something was up with her latest customers, but she didn't probe. Jessie needed to make sure that they could now make the Inn on Charlotte their headquarters and could depend on her secrecy.

"Miss Claudia, thank you for being so kind to us. But we have a very important favor to ask of you," Jessie said after she sat down in one of the empty seats. "We need to make your B & B our headquarters, if you will. And we need to know that we can trust you to secrecy should you overhear us. We're in a very delicate situation. We have people after us who want us dead, who want my girl dead, and now you. There are too many innocent people in this. Can we count on you?" His last question was more of a statement than a question. He watched her carefully gauging her response.

She nodded that she understood, then stood up and said, "Well, if that's all gentlemen, I'll just go about my everyday normal business like usual." She looked Jessie straight in the eyes. He knew she understood. "Is there anything I can get for you?"

"Breakfast in bed for the lady in my room." She nodded. Jessie could tell that request caught her more off guard than the idea of someone wanting her dead. But she just nodded and then went about her business as usual, as she had said.

He turned to his cousins. "Let's fill the guys in." Jessie started from the beginning. "We think we can get close enough to Rudy to kill him. But it involves putting Gracie at risk. Our idea is to get Gracie to enter the mansion through the servants' quarters. She's going to need to decide whom she can trust and whom she is going to bring into this operation. The servants know more than anyone else about what is going on in that house. With that information, we'll determine a more secure plan on killing Rudy, but we're going to somehow pin it on Phillip Proctor. We're also going to take Timmy. With the election being a week away, and both Rudy and Phillip being back home from the campaign trail, we're afraid they will try to do something to Timmy to get Gracie to come out of hiding. But again, Gracie and the servants are the main players here."

"Boss, it's a great idea!" Clyde said. "We'll just take some added precautions when it comes to Gracie. But she can do this. She's a natural, as we've been telling ya! We need to go forward with this."

Bubba was very protective of Gracie and while he agreed it was a great plan, he didn't want her to have to do it. Especially almost five months pregnant. "Maybe we should ask Gracie what she thinks. See if she's willing to do it," although he already knew she would be. She was tough, tougher than anyone knew.

They sat around the table, talking about the extra

precautions they could take when it came to Gracie getting into the servants' quarters. Choosing servants to bring into their operation would be solely Gracie's responsibility. She knew them, and they knew her. Only she could decide that part of their plan. But the guys would run every precautionary background check on the servants she picked just to be sure they were trustworthy.

And then there was Phillip Proctor. He was back in Orlando after being on the campaign trail, angry as a disturbed hornet's nest. None of his contacts in any state knew where Conners had taken Gracie. He also had his police officer whom he paid to call all his contacts in different states, but still no word of Gracie or Conners. Phillip was frequenting the house more often than usual since the campaign was the upcoming week.

The election was approaching. It was the first week of March and everyone working on the campaign was working overtime. That meant that the mansion was overwhelmed with campaign workers. The longer Jessie and everyone waited, and the closer they got to the election, the more people they chanced getting injured. All Rudy and Phillip did at this point were public appearances.

Gracie's mother was still in the hospital. And Timmy was locked inside the house.

* * *

Gracie arose to a quiet knock on the door to her suite and the smile of a lovely lady with a tray of food. Gracie instantly liked her. "Hi, ma'am," she said. "Sorry to wake you, but I figured you must be famished after that car ride yesterday." Clearly, Jessie had her in the loop.

Gracie sat up, holding the covers since she was

naked. "Yes ma'am, I am!" she replied lazily.

Claudia introduced herself and set the tray next to Gracie. "If there is anything you need while you are here, anything at all, you just let me know. My bedroom is on the third floor, but if you just pick up the phone and dial star three, you'll get me if you can't find me."

Gracie smiled and thanked the nice woman before settling in and devouring her breakfast. She decided to dress and venture out after she finished. She could make out distinctly male voices coming from the front of the B & B. She knew Jessie would be out there.

She put on her jeans from yesterday. She grabbed a fresh t-shirt out of her luggage and ran a quick brush through her hair. Her t-shirt fit snuggly around her waist. There was no hiding the pregnancy. She looked almost full term instead of five months pregnant. Her hair was going in every which direction and crowding her face, but after last night, she really didn't care. So she pulled it up into a messy bun with tendrils slipping out around her face and the nape of her neck. She slipped on some flip-flops and headed into the breakfast room. Funny how she missed her warm sweaters and flannel pajamas already.

Jessie's back was to her, but he saw in his cousins' reactions that she must have walked in behind him. Gracie was a little taken aback that there were new guys she had never met. Instinctively, she backed up a few paces; put her arms around her stomach. She searched Jessie's face for reassurance when he turned around.

"Gracie, these are my cousins," Jessie explained. "They're going to help us with this." Immediately, Gracie let her guard down. Introductions were made, and then she sat down.

Gavin went over the basics of their plan, but then prepared for an afternoon of questioning Gracie about the household servants needed to complete it.

"So you really believe you can just walk into the servants' quarters and no one will see you?" Gavin asked.

"The quarters are around back of the property. They're not attached to the house. The only servants' quarters that are attached to the house are the nannies', cooks', and security's. But I can get word from the maids' quarters at the back of the property to the nannies attached to the house in one day. I know exactly who we can trust." That's what everyone was counting on. "I only have one request," she added.

"Anything," Jessie pleaded, feeling sicker by the minute as he sat and listened to how Gracie was going to put herself and their baby in danger.

"After each servant has done their part in this, they are going to become a part of us. I'm using my most trustworthy servants, who are like family to me. If they stay in the house, they will surely be killed. Every one that helps us, comes with us."

That sounded reasonable enough to Jessie. "Absolutely," he said. She smiled at him, that beautiful smile, and he put an arm around her back, gently rubbing it as she was filled in on the details.

Gavin continued, "I really think we should make our move Monday night. We'll make our way around the back of property during shift change for the guards. Gracie, you'll go into the servants' quarters and look for your maid. Wait for your guard to make his way to the back entrance of the property, and then come outside with her, and go straight to the guard. Tell the guard and maid what you need. They will be our first two accomplices. They will need to get word to your nanny and Timmy's nanny that we need to speak with them the following night. Tuesday, we'll do the same, just arrive a little later, so the guard, maid, and nannies will already be waiting for us. Then we go from there and gather as much information as we can."

Gracie nodded in approval. She looked at Jessie. "This will work. Gavin's really good at fitting all the pieces together. This is actually going to work!" she exclaimed, excited to show off her newfound skills at being a part of a hit team, even if she was pregnant.

Jessie nodded in agreement. "Tomorrow's Sunday. We'll take it off and rest up, in case anyone's watching. We'll meet up here, Monday afternoon. Come leisurely, when you can make your getaway from your hotels. But remember, we have to be at the property at ten pm. It's a two-hour drive from here."

Everyone nodded in agreement, which lead them into some leisurely conversations. Jessie stood up and whispered in Gracie's ear for her to follow him back to their room. She did so obediently.

Once behind closed doors, he walked up to her and kissed her again, leaving her lips red and swollen. "I don't want you to do this. Let me do this for you," he pleaded.

She shook her head. "I can do this. And I wouldn't do it if I felt like Gavin's plan had me too close to danger."

He didn't know what else to say. Everyone supported the plan, and Gracie agreed to do it. He could only keep the closest eye on her, to make sure nothing happened to her. He sat on the edge of the bed and pulled her into his lap. He wrapped his arms around her. "When I told you I intended for us to have a life together, I meant it," he continued. "I want you to be mine forever."

She smiled and wrapped her fingers around his. "I believed you back then, and I want the same thing."

She was silent for a second. "Who would have thought back in November, I'd fall in love with the same man who robbed and abducted me?" They both laughed.

Chapter Fourteen

Gracie had no problem falling asleep, but Jessie stayed awake for most of the night, cursing himself for putting her in this situation. He didn't want her back on the Talbot's property. But he couldn't deny that she was the key to their eventual safety.

Monday morning proved to be cold, damp, and rainy. They ate breakfast in bed, and then prepared a bag for their trip to Orlando. Gracie was apprehensive, yet ready for action. She had been mentally preparing herself since she found Jessie's note in the room off of the loft that she would one day participate in their hits. Now was her time to shine, to show everyone just what she was made of.

No one wanted Rudy Talbot dead more than she did. It wasn't going to be hard convincing the staff to help either. They didn't like the man any better than she did, especially her people – the ones she considered family because they had always treated her so kindly growing up. Those were the staff members she would include in their mission and then bring along with her. She felt like she owed them a better life than they would have serving in the Orlando mansion.

Slowly, the guys arrived at Claudia's B & B. She never said a word about their proceedings, but seemed to understand they'd need a big dinner and snacks for the road. She prepared an early dinner.

Pot roast with vegetables and chocolate cake for
afterwards. Then, as she finished clearing off the
tables while they went over their plan one last time,
she brought a bag out to Gracie and whispered in
her ear, "Make sure to keep your stomach full! You
don't want hungry stomachs giving you away."
Claudia smiled at her, then retreated back to the
kitchen. Gracie was extremely thankful.

While the rest of the guys loaded up the two
trucks they would take on their mission, Gracie
retreated back into their bedroom to dress for the
night. She wore dark jeans, a long sleeved black
shirt, and a black men's sweatshirt with a hoodie
that hid her figure. She pulled her hair back into a
bun, and grabbed a black winter cap to pull over it
when they got there. It was important for her former
staff to see her face, so she left the ski mask in the
suitcase. She had a gun concealed in the waist of her
jeans, and one attached to her left ankle in case
there were any problems.

She and Jessie finished getting dressed, and then
headed to the parking lot. Both were too nervous to
talk. They were the last members of the group to load
into the truck, and then they headed South on I-95
towards Orlando.

* * *

As they approached the city, Gracie couldn't help but
feel like she had never left. All the landmarks were so
familiar and she used to sneak into the house by way
of the back property gate when she was a teenager.
In that respect, what she was doing tonight didn't
seem dangerous at all. She had done it for years.

The two black Tahoes turned off their lights and
pulled off the main roads. They started down the
back alleys behind the other mansions in the

neighborhood. Only the maintenance, trash, and recycling people took these roads. Gracie unbuckled her seat belt, sitting forward to direct Derek where to go. Once they got to the Talbot's property line, Derek slowed and drove just past it, parking before the gate in case they needed a quick getaway. The other Tahoe was right behind them.

Jessie pulled her close and kissed her. "Are you ready for this?"

"Yes," she said. She moved past him and out of the SUV. Jessie left the door open, crouched in the entrance, so he could keep an eye on her at all times.

She moved through the hedges like she had been practicing this her whole life. In one way, she had been. Sneaking in and out of the house during her rebellious teenage years had paid off. She knew where the security cameras covered and where they didn't. She waited behind one hedge and watched the revolving camera at the back property entrance. It brought back so many memories. She waited until she knew she wasn't in the camera's sight, and then slipped between the pickets of the wrought iron gates. The gates were no match for any intruders. The pickets were too widely spaced apart. Anyone could just walk right in. A security measure Rudy gravely overlooked.

Once inside the gates, the darkness swallowed her and she was out of Jessie's sight. He left the van and took the same route she did, but waited behind the last shrub outside of the property.

Gracie ran straight for the servants' quarters. She knew the pass code, entered it, and the front door swung wide open. She was inside before the security camera could turn back in the other direction to see her. She was fast.

She wasn't sure who would be on the other side of the door, so she made sure to keep one hand on her pistol. But no one was in the entry.

The entry hall was just that, a long hallway with rooms on either side. It was painted a dull cream with cream tile on the floor. There was no color or warmth to the quarters. To her immediate left was a living room the servants sometimes gathered during their time off, and the kitchen was on the right. Both were empty. It was just after ten pm. The servants were usually in their rooms, which were off of the hallway as well. She hoped that the servants had the same rooms as they did when Gracie lived there.

Moving silently down the hall, she made her way to Maid Annie's room, the fourth door on the left.

She listened outside for a moment and heard shuffling of feet inside. Slowly she opened the door. It was Annie's room. A bit startled, Annie turned around to find a disguised Gracie closing the door behind her.

"Miss Gracie!" she exclaimed. Even with her hair hidden, her distinct facial features gave her away immediately.

"Shhhh!" Gracie quickly silenced her. "No one can know I'm here!"

Annie was shocked to see her. Rudy had a "meeting" where he told everyone Gracie was dead, but they didn't want the public to know just yet since they were still trying to capture her killers. But here she was, in the flesh and blood. And something was different about her, but Annie couldn't quite put her finger on it.

"I need your help," Gracie said closing the gap between them. She took Annie's hands and sat down on the edge of the bed with her.

"But you're supposed to be dead!" Annie exclaimed in a hushed voice.

"Is that what Rudy's telling everyone?" she asked.

"Yes. He told us shortly after you disappeared."

"What a bastard!" she let out under her breath, then reminded herself to stay on track. "Well clearly I'm not! And I need your help! But you should know it's dangerous."

Annie just nodded her head. "Anything for you Miss Gracie!"

Annie had been Gracie's personal maid since she was born. Annie was more of a mother figure to her than her own mother had been. Annie cleaned up every mess before Rudy could find it and take his frustrations out on her. Annie had a knack for knowing when he was in close quarters.

"Is Henry still the nighttime security guard?" Gracie asked.

"Yes."

"We need to go outside and meet Henry. But we can't let anyone see us. Can we go through your window?" Gracie asked getting up and heading over to it. "Turn out the lights."

Annie did just that. The servant's windows were wired to the security system. She needed to make sure that they undid the top security bar and tape it to the bottom bar, so when she lifted the window, the security system wouldn't sound an alarm concerning an open window. It was still too cold to open the windows, even for Florida. Whoever was on security would think it odd for a window to be open and Gracie couldn't take the chance that they would come investigate to find out why.

"How did you learn how to do that?" Annie asked astonished.

She kept her voice down, but let out a tiny laugh. "This I've known how to do for years. I've been sneaking in and out of this place through my bedroom window for as long as I can remember!"

Gracie's suite had double doors that lead out to a veranda. Although she was on the third floor, ivy climbed the trellis that reached up the three stories. Night after night, Gracie used to climb over the ledge to her balcony and climb down the trellis. She'd run across the lawn under the cover of darkness, say a quick hello to Henry, and then dart out of the gate to meet her friends. Not the socialites her mother made her visit. Her real friends. The ones she went to bonfire parties with and drank away the pain of her latest beating. She truly was a rebellious socialite.

Gracie knew even Jessie would be impressed. And she was starting to realize just how important she was to this job. She was sure the guys knew how to keep from tripping a security system, but she knew the ins and outs of the entire property. She was the crucial member in this particular hit and she was proud of that.

Jessie watched as Gracie helped Annie out of the window, then climbed out herself. They waited by the side of the house until they saw Henry approach the gate and take his position for the night, right in front of the security camera. She knew that Henry would assess the gate, and then walk the premises. There were only two areas where the security camera would not pick them up. She hurried Annie to the bushes inside the gate adjacent to the building. She whispered for Annie to memorize the exact path they had taken and pay attention to everything they were doing. She was going to have to do it again every night until they had completed their mission. Then they walked between the bushes and the brick wall, hidden by the heavy foliage to the edge of the gate. She saw Jessie crouched down on the other side.

Gracie and Annie waited until Henry started to approach. The security cameras did have night vision, but did not have sound. Another security mistake Rudy overlooked. As Henry approached, Gracie waited until he was far enough to the left of the security gate to be out of the security cameras' view. Then she whispered to Annie to call out to Henry.

"Annie, what in the world are you doing in the bushes?" he asked.

"We're stepping out," she whispered. Gracie was right behind her. She looked to Jessie on the other side of the gate and motioned for him to come out as well.

"Gracie?" Henry asked in astonishment. "Is that you?"

"Hey Henry!" she said, giving him a big hug. Henry let Gracie get away with sneaking in and out of the house for all those years. She owed him big time! He covered for her on many close calls.

"But Rudy said..." he trailed off as he caught sight of Jessie standing on just the other side of an iron gate that provided no protection. He was a menacing sight. In the dark, Jessie looked dangerous. He was tall, muscular, and his shadow was even bigger than he was. Henry went to put his hand on his gun, but Jessie was quick to reach through the gate and grab the gun faster than Henry could. By the time Henry's hand reached where the gun should be, Jessie was holding it, pointing it towards the ground.

"I know Rudy told you I was dead, but I'm not. And these guys aren't here to hurt anybody, they're here to help," Gracie said squeezing Henry's hand. She hadn't realized how much she missed her friends, her family really. "Henry, we need your help. This is Jessie. He's in charge of this whole thing. I need you guys to trust him."

Henry was so relieved to see Gracie alive, he'd do just about anything she asked. But he recognized Jessie as the lead person who had abducted Gracie and wasn't sure if she was being pressured into this.

"Miss Gracie, how do I know you're doing this on

your own free will and this man isn't forcing you?"

She hadn't counted on Henry giving her a hard time. Then again, he was a security guard because of his keen instincts. It was his job to question, and then question again.

"Because Rudy tried to have me killed and this man and his guys saved my life. Because I'm in love with him and I'm five months pregnant with his baby." She stated it simply, but the easiness of those words surprised her even more than the looks on Henry and Annie's faces.

"Ok!" Henry said. "I'm in." Just hearing that Rudy tried to hurt her was enough for him to participate.

"We don't have a lot of time. Annie," she said addressing both of them, "we need to know everything that is going on in the house. Who comes, who goes, when, where, everything. Put together a schedule for me for the next week. Break into Rudy's office if you have to, but we need it to be as accurate as possible." Annie and Henry nodded in approval.

"What are you going to do with that information?" Henry asked.

Gracie looked at Jessie to get the nod of approval to tell them their plan. He gave it. "We're going to abduct Timmy, kill Rudy, and pin it on Phillip. Then we're going to take you and any other servant in this house that helps me along with us when we're done." It took them both a few moments to absorb the dangerous actions they were being asked to be a part of. But neither one backed down. "We know what happens when they are out of the house. We need to know their daily schedules and routines inside the house."

"It shouldn't be hard to get you that information," Annie said quietly.

"Where's Timmy?" She'd been waiting so long to ask that question.

Annie and Henry exchanged glances. "He's being kept under house arrest. He can't leave his quarters. He hasn't spoken a word since Rudy told him you were killed."

Gracie's breath caught in her throat and Jessie stepped through the iron gates to put a hand behind her back. The loving action made Henry understand the relationship between him and Gracie. And it was this understanding that allowed Henry to put his faith in Jessie and their plan.

Gracie had all but lost her footing. With Jessie's support, she was able to stay standing and regain her composure.

Jessie issued a warning. "Timmy can't know anything yet. If he knows Gracie is still alive, his disposition will change, and we can't risk Rudy or Phillip seeing any changes in the house. The house must stay exactly as it is, or we'll never be able to get close enough to kill him. And trust me, if we don't get to him, he'll get to us, to Timmy. It's just a matter of time. If anyone hears of any plans to hurt Timmy or sees Timmy being hurt, notify us immediately!"

Both Henry and Annie knew he was right. Gracie did too on her subconscious level, but she was looking toward the house and Jessie knew exactly what she was thinking. "Not tonight. But soon enough. He'll be fine Gracie," Jessie said.

"Who can we trust that's closest to Timmy?" Jessie asked the three of them, bringing her back into their conversation.

Annie frowned. "Your nanny was fired and Rudy found her a position out of state."

"What about Melissa?" Gracie inquired. Any time Gracie couldn't be there, Melissa was second in line.

Annie nodded. "She has replaced your nanny, but Timmy hasn't taken to her. She can be trusted though. She's trying her hardest with him."

Gracie was so happy to hear that, she made a special mental note to someday repay Melissa for the kindness and energy she spent on Timmy during this time.

Gracie faced Jessie. "Melissa will do."

Jessie continued, "Henry, Annie, I need you to get word to Melissa to meet us here, same time tomorrow night. Annie, can you remember the exact route Gracie took you on to get you here?" She nodded yes. "Come the exact same way with Melissa. Make sure you let her know that Gracie's alive, but no one else is to know. Not even Timmy. We need to talk to her tomorrow night. Remember, same time, same place. And bring that schedule. We're going to stay on the other side of the fence. It's safer for Gracie if we need to get away."

As Jessie finished speaking, Henry's walkie-talkie went off with the sound of another man's voice. "Everything alright, Henry? I don't have a visual."

Jessie nodded at both Annie and Henry. They understood that they were done for the night. They had been given their assignments, and if they were kept any longer, someone might suspect something.

"I'm fine. Just seeing a man about a dog." Henry lied easily. He and Jessie exchanged smiles as he helped Gracie back through the wrought iron gates. Annie retreated back behind the bushes, and Jessie held out Henry's gun once they were on the other side. Taking it, Henry went back to work.

Gracie and Jessie made their way back to the truck. Once inside, Derek pulled away. No one said anything until they were on I-95 North heading back to St. Augustine. Gracie just stared out the window. Jessie knew she was thinking of Timmy. It was going to be very hard for her not to take him right away. She was so worried they would hurt him. But she needed to stay strong. Jessie hadn't planned on stepping in tonight, but Gracie needed him. It became clear that she couldn't be alone during these nightly encounters, or any other part of this plan. He'd have to stay with her.

She just stared out the window the entire two hours back to the B & B. It was close to two am and she was exhausted and distraught. Jessie took her into their room, then excused himself to go help the guys put the trucks away. He really needed time to tell them about what had transpired tonight. Gracie wandered into the bathroom, and turned on the water for a hot bath. She needed time to think and was chilled to the bone. A hot bath would help her think and sooth her nerves.

Chapter Fifteen

Gracie finished her bath before Jessie got back into the room. She put on one of his shirts and crawled into bed. She was asleep before her head hit the pillow. Jessie stayed up late briefing the guys about Henry and Annie. He had Clyde looking into them to make sure they were trustworthy sources. He had confidence in Gracie's choices but he wouldn't take any chances.

Everyone slept in the next morning. Tuesday proved to be just as dreary as Monday. It was the start of the rainy season, before the weather turned to summer for the next nine months. Jessie woke around lunchtime, when he heard his guys in the main part of the house. Today, he didn't get up and go out to them. Gracie was snuggled against his side and rolled in the middle of the night to use his arm as her pillow. He lost feeling in his arm hours ago, but he wasn't about to move it. So he just lay there until he felt her stirring next to him.

They prepared the same as the previous day. Again, Claudia had an early dinner ready with snacks for the night. Gracie said nothing throughout the day. She was waiting for Gavin. He was the one who made these plans. And she intended on telling him just what she thought of his plan with Timmy.

Gavin, Landon, and Luka had never seen Gracie's fiery temper. It could be turned on and off like the flick of a switch. When Gavin casually walked into the B & B, Gracie flew out of her seat toward him. Sending her chair flying backwards, Gracie had a hold of Gavin's shirt collar pinning him against the wall in a matter of seconds. Gracie was a force to be reckoned with even while pregnant.

"Change of plans!" she shouted at Gavin. She was pissed. And Gavin, who seemed to be the one keeping her from her brother, was going to get the brunt of her mood.

Gavin's instincts told him to grab a hold of Gracie's hands, and turn her wrists for her to let go of him. But a quick glance at Jessie told him to think differently. So he let her pin him against the wall and prepared to take whatever she was going to give him.

"We get Timmy tonight. No exceptions! So figure out a plan that revolves around that. With you or without you, I'm going in the house and I'm getting him. Figure it out or I'll do it for you."

It took Gavin a second to understand what she was saying. "Ok. We'll figure something out, but you have to let me go," Gavin said. Bubba, as usual, overly emotional, couldn't help but laugh as Gracie let go of his shirt collar.

"Gracie's pissed," Bubba whispered to Clyde. Clyde shot him the death look, but Bubba knew Gracie wouldn't care if he laughed at her pinning someone three times her size against the wall.

She kept her gaze down, oblivious that everyone was staring at her. She sat down and laid out the plan she came up with while in the tub the night before. "Melissa will be at the gate. Annie will show her how to get there. The nannies make a nightly round around eleven pm. We'll have enough time to talk to her, Annie and Henry. Melissa will wait there while I do her nightly rounds. The nanny is always the last one awake in the children's quarters. No one will think anything of me being in there." She paused for a moment making sure everyone was keeping up with her.

Gavin liked the sound of this plan but knew it needed some tweaking. And he knew Jessie certainly did not like this plan. "Gracie, do you think you can get us all into the house unnoticed?"

She thought a second. "If I don't trade places with Melissa tonight, and we brief her of our plan, so she can get word to the servants inside the house tomorrow, then yes. That would mean on Wednesday, we'd enter the house. But I don't think I can wait one more day for Timmy!"

"I don't like it!" Jessie said, unsurprised by everyone.

"Jessie, I have to get in there. Timmy isn't going to go with Melissa. He doesn't trust her. It has to be me. And I am the only one that can get you guys inside without being noticed. The staff will know you're there if we have Melissa spread the word, so if they see you, which they will in order to get you into the house, they won't be alarmed. Once inside, I can lead you to wherever you want to go."

Gracie's plan put everything into motion much more quickly than anticipated. But Gavin liked it. It was the quickest and surest way to get Timmy, the servants, and themselves out of harm's way. And with the election in five days, they were running out of time. This gave them a direct route to Rudy Talbot and Phillip Proctor.

"We'll need to brief Melissa tonight, and wait until Wednesday, Gracie. You can hold out one more day. We have to know who's in the house and all the details of what is going on Wednesday. We need that schedule to know when Rudy and Phillip will be inside the house. We'll have to plan our execution perfectly, or it won't work," Gavin added.

Gracie wasn't patient and she didn't like the idea of waiting, but she would if she had to. And she knew she did. "Alright, I will brief Annie, Henry, and Melissa tonight. We'll get all the information. Tomorrow we'll go over how to get you guys in the house. Then we'll decide what we want to do once we're in there."

Everyone gave their approval except Jessie. "The only way I'm going to go along with this is if I'm by Gracie's side every second."

"Fine," Gavin said to appease him for the moment. "It'll put Gracie at more risk to be seen with you, the face of the person who supposedly killed her. But if you're that insistent, then fine."

Jessie cursed under his breath and left the table, slamming the bedroom door behind him. Gracie just let him go. There was nothing she could say to change his mind, and Gavin was exactly right. But apparently, that was a risk they were going to have to take.

* * *

Nighttime came quickly and once again Gracie found herself in the black Tahoe headed toward Orlando. The anticipation was getting to Gracie tonight, and she couldn't sit still. Jessie had been in a sour mood all day. Everyone else was strictly business. If they couldn't get all the information they needed tonight, they would have to wait another. And every night they kept this up, they had a greater chance of being found out and killed. And they only had a few more nights until Election Day. They couldn't risk Phillip or Rudy doing something to Timmy to bring Gracie out of hiding right before the election. They also couldn't risk either one of them getting elected. It would give them too much power and protection.

They approached the gate, and Derek pulled just past it as he did the previous night. Gracie gave Jessie a kiss, then pulled the cap over her hair. She ran the same course she did the previous night and already saw Henry walking towards the left side of the gate.

"Henry, it's me," Gracie said as she stayed hidden in the dark shadows of the tall shrubs on the outside of the property. Jessie could see her outline from the truck. He stayed where he was. "Where's Annie and Melissa?"

"We're here!" Annie whispered as she and Melissa stepped out from behind the shrubs on the inside of the gate. They only had a few minutes before the security guard watching the cameras would get suspicious about Henry being out of sight again.

"Miss Gracie, I am so glad you're ok!" Melissa said.

"So am I Melissa! It's so good to see you! Did Annie and Henry explain everything?" Gracie quickly asked.

"Yes," she said.

"There's been a slight change of plans. Melissa, I need to know everything that is going on inside the house tomorrow too."

Melissa hesitated. "I only know of some of the events. I'd have to ask around to get a complete itinerary."

Damn, Gracie thought. "Ok. Can you do that tonight? Can you alert everyone that they are not to make a scene about any of this? Tell them that I'm alive and that there is going to be some commotion possibly tomorrow or during the next few days, but they are to go about their business as usual. If they see someone strange inside the house, do not be alarmed and just pretend like they didn't see a thing. Can you remember all that?"

Melissa quickly nodded her head yes.

Before she could go on, Henry's radio went off again, giving them less time than the night before. She cursed under her breath. "Henry, what is going on with you? I've lost visual again."

Henry answered his call. "Sorry, I think I'm getting a urinary tract infection. May have to call on the doctor tomorrow. Give me one more second. Everything alright on the cameras?" It was a genius question to ask. Gracie could hear if the man inside, who was hand picked by Rudy to keep tabs of all surveillance videos, suspected anything.

"The same two trucks pulled past the property gates again. Did you see them? Do you still have visual of them?"

Henry was a good liar. "No. I think they belong to the Bently's. They're having some work done on their servants' quarters."

"At night?" the security guy asked.

"They're delivering materials at night so the workers can start in the mornings. At least that's what I've seen," Henry lied again.

"Alright. Let me know if they cause you any trouble. I'm out."

"Over and out," Henry said.

"Miss Gracie, I've got to go. He's not giving me much time."

"I understand," she said. "Melissa and Annie, alert everyone, and find out a complete itinerary of tomorrow's proceedings. Do you think you can send me word at the Inn on Charlotte in St. Augustine?"

They both looked a little confused, but they nodded in agreement.

"We'll have it to you by morning," Annie said as they stepped back behind the bushes and departed. Henry gave her a nod and turned back to walk the premises under the watchful eye of Big Brother.

Gracie turned and left as she watched the camera

to make sure her retreat was timed just right. When she entered the truck, Derek sped off. She took off her cap, let her hair down, and swore like a drunken sailor.

"The surveillance guy hardly gave us any time. Melissa was there, but she's not sure of tomorrow's events. She and Annie are going to spread the word, and they are going to send a message to me at the B & B in the morning of the itinerary for tomorrow. That's the best we could do with the time given." She was disappointed and discouraged. How many more nights was she going to have to go through like this until they entered the house? Apparently, one more.

"You did great!" Jessie said grabbing her with both hands and kissing her. He didn't let her go for several seconds.

"There's another thing. Big Brother has noticed the trucks. We'll have to back into the alley tomorrow night so we don't go past the back gate. Henry made up some excuse about the neighbors having work done, but we need to proceed cautiously."

"Gracie, you did really great," Gavin chimed in. "We'll figure out in the morning what we have to do tomorrow night."

Once again, Gracie spent the rest of the car ride staring out the window. She drew herself a warm bath when they got back to their room while Jessie stayed outside to talk to the guys. She was lost in her thoughts when Jessie knocked on the bathroom door and came inside.

"You ok?" he asked, sitting on the edge of the tub.

She shrugged her shoulders. "Rudy's apparently got a tight rein on everyone. We hardly had two minutes to talk. He's really got a control problem and it seems to have spread to the staff as well. This could be a big problem."

He took his shirt off and stood up to slide off his

jeans.

"What are you doing?" Gracie asked with a smile.

He climbed in the bathtub, sending water spilling out over the side. "You need a distraction!" he said teasingly.

"Oh yeah? And just what exactly would that entail?" she teased back.

He kissed her gently, then again, and again with more force and passion. She kissed him back each time, matching the intensity of the kiss. She knew what kind of distraction he was talking about, and she was thankful to have it.

Chapter Sixteen

The next morning, Gracie awoke early, anxious to see if Annie and Melissa sent word to her yet. By 10 am, Gracie was pacing the dining room, with Jessie and his cousins watching her. Just then, Claudia poked her head through the door holding the cordless phone.

"Gracie," she whispered, "phone's for you." Before she even finished her sentence, Gracie grabbed the phone out of her hand. She pressed speakerphone so the guys could hear.

"I'm here," Gracie said.

It was Annie. "Nothing of importance this morning. Melissa will keep the normal nanny schedule. You remember, right?" she asked. Gracie nodded yes. "Four pm the master has a meeting with the media again. Six pm dinner with Phillip Proctor. After, they are to retire to his office to talk business. Should take a couple of hours. Phillip usually doesn't leave until ten or eleven pm."

"Anyone else in the house?" Gracie asked. Gavin was taking notes.

"The priest is always here for dinner and sometimes sits in on the meetings, but not always. There's no way to tell."

Gracie knew she had to keep it short. "Tell Melissa to pack Timmy a bag with warm clothes and some of his things. Keep it light if you can. Hide it under the foot of his bed but don't let him see you. Put him to bed by eight." Annie agreed. "Great job, Annie. Make sure to pack a bag for yourself and Melissa too."

Annie hung up the phone and Gracie looked up at Jessie and Gavin. Their minds were at work planning tonight's events. But this time, they included Gracie.

"What time can we enter the house?" they asked her.

She thought for a moment. "Nine pm. Timmy will be in bed and most of the servants will be finishing up for the day, so it will minimize the amount of people in the house. Who all is planning on going inside?"

"Derek and Peter will stay with the vans. Henry will stay outside with them. Everyone else goes in." Gavin said.

Gracie thought for another moment. "Best way to go in is through the attached servants' quarters. There is a door that connects to the kitchen. The cooks will be finishing up the dishes, but if Melissa has briefed them, then they shouldn't be alarmed if we enter the house that way." Gracie proceeded to draw out a map of the entire house. She included every door, every floorboard that creaked and moaned, and every escape route possible if something went wrong. By that time, Gavin had the plan figured out in his head, and all the guys had gathered at the B & B.

"Alright, before we enter, Clyde will cut the power to the street. They won't think something is amiss if the entire street has a black out. We'll need flashlights, but dim ones. We don't want to give ourselves away. We'll enter in through the kitchen, and take the servants staircase to the second floor. Gracie, you'll leave through the servants' door on the second floor into Timmy's quarters. It'd be best if you had him out of the house before we even get to

Rudy's office. So we'll wait for you to grab him and his bag. Once you bring him back through the door, we'll proceed with our part of it, but you need to haul ass with Timmy and get him back to the truck as quickly as possible!"

Gracie nodded that she understood. "What about you, Jessie?"

"Jessie will take us straight to Rudy's office." Jessie knew where it was because of his past dealings with Rudy. "There will be no surveillance, so we'll go out through Timmy's room. Once inside the office, we know what to do." Gavin was going to leave out the rest. It was more complicated than Gracie knew and they were not going to get her involved in that portion of their plan. They had made a pact early in the planning of this particular mission to not tell her about what would go on inside the office. She just didn't need to know.

"Melissa, Annie, and Henry will be waiting for us at the gate. I'm going to lead them into the trucks first. Then you all can follow me into the house." Gracie added. Everyone seemed ok with that.

"The house has a back up generator," she went on. "Big Brother surveillance man, whoever the hell he is, is going to have to go outside to the far right of the property to turn it on. We'll be on a time crunch, and he'll have to cross the lawn. We need to try to get into the servants' quarters very quickly, and up to the stairs to Timmy's room. We'll have about five minutes from the time the generator is turned back on until Big Brother is back at his station watching the surveillance cameras. So don't panic immediately if the lights come back on." This was why Gracie was so important to this mission. She was the only one with this kind of information.

They went over a few more details, but had the plan squared away by mid-afternoon. By four o'clock, they were all gathered around the television to watch Rudy's latest press conference.

Chief Brunnell stood alongside Rudy and the Catholic priest. "This morning we were called to the house of Rudy Talbot. A ransom note was faxed to Mr. Talbot asking for more money and threatening the life of Timmy Talbot, Mr. Talbot's son, should he still choose to run for State Attorney General."

"What about Gracie? Is she presumed dead at this point?" A reporter asked.

"Yes. At this point, we presume that Gracie is dead," the Chief answered.

"What's being done to find Timmy?" another reporter asked.

"We've already issued an Amber Alert. A tipster told us he saw two White Explorers pulling away from the back entrance of the Talbot's property last night. White Explorers, matching the description of the SUV's Gracie was abducted in. We believe those were the cars he was taken in. If you have seen anything unusual in the neighborhood, please contact us immediately. We are still offering monetary rewards leading to information about Gracie and Timmy Talbot."

The Chief turned and helped guide Rudy down the stairs and off the podium. Jessie turned off the TV as the priest began a prayer.

"Gracie, Annie said he had a press conference scheduled. This was planned. Remember what we talked about."

Gracie shook her head and took two puffs of her inhaler. She knew this was their last ditch effort to bring her out of hiding.

"I know, I know," she said. "It's just hard to hear."

Jessie hugged her. "You know Annie and Melissa would have told us if something happened to Timmy."

She nodded her head. "I think I need to go lie down and try to relax."

"I think that's a good idea," Jessie said.

Gracie got up and walked back to her room. Jessie followed right behind her.

"You know," Jessie said trying to cheer her up, "we've decided it would be too dangerous to come back here. So we're going to head back to the mountains," Jessie said casually.

"Are you serious?" she asked, excited at the thought. She missed the cozy cabin, the view from the upstairs bedroom, and her dogs. God, she missed those dogs.

"We'll have to pack up before we leave. When you grab Timmy, make sure he has a few comfort items," Jessie said, thinking of what it would be like for him to be plucked out of his home.

Gracie's heart melted at the way Jessie was thinking about Timmy. "You know he's only five. He's still just a kid. We're going to be raising him," she added, not quite sure if Jessie realized that. "And we'll have a nanny, maid, and security officer living with us as well as your three cousins. Are you sure the cabin's big enough?"

"My guys will be building a few smaller cabins around the property come spring. There will be plenty of room. We need a security officer at the gate anyway if we're going to have a little one running around outside. I'm hoping that just the three of us and Timmy," Jessie said putting a hand on Gracie's belly, "will be the only ones in our cabin."

She had never thought about that. What it would be like to just be with him. She instantly liked the idea.

But Jessie was hesitating and Gracie knew that he had something of importance he wanted to say, but didn't know how to say it. "Gracie, this is dangerous, you know that. Phillip will do anything to get to you and Rudy will let him. There's a good chance someone is going to get hurt." She had been keeping that thought far from entering her mind. But he brought it up, and now she thought of what he meant by that comment.

She smiled. If this was going to be their last hours together, she wasn't about to spend them crying over something that might not happen.

Sitting on the edge of the bed, Gracie walked over to Jessie and stood between his legs. She wrapped her arms around his neck and gave him a gentle kiss. Jessie ran his hands along her sides, grabbing her hips and pulling her closer to him.

Gracie let go of Jessie's neck and pulled his shirt over his head. She let her hands roam down his chest muscles for a moment, then pushed him backwards onto the bed. Falling on his elbows with his legs still bent over the side of the bed he watched Gracie.

With deliberate slowness, she took off each flip-flop. Next, she crossed her arms, grabbing the bottom of her t-shirt and pulled it over her head, letting it drop to the floor. She pulled her jeans down her legs and stepped out of them. She kept her eyes locked on Jessie's and could see his breathing start to quicken. She could also see his need for her growing under his jeans.

Even more slowly, Gracie took off her bra. Her breasts had begun to swell from the pregnancy and Jessie wanted to feel their fullness in his hands. He tried to sit up, but Gracie pushed him back down on his elbows. After she slid her panties to the floor, she unbuttoned Jessie's jeans and pulled them off, followed by his boxers.

She climbed on top of him, each knee resting on either side of Jessie.

Still keeping eye contact with him, Gracie slowly lowered herself to take him in. Jessie's eyes darkened with his need to have her. When she took all of him in her, Jessie let himself lay on his back and groaned with pleasure.

Gracie took charge, sliding along Jessie as he gripped the comforter behind his head. Gracie was sure to keep a slow and steady pace, to drive him wild. She succeeded. Jessie grabbed her waist and changed the pace to fast and hard. This time it was Gracie who gasped with pleasure.

They both climaxed together. Gracie was out of breath and Jessie couldn't seem to stop moving inside her.

"Jessie," she gasped, "I have to stop. I can't take anymore!" She was exhausted and he had worn her out.

He moaned, but then pulled her up and off of him, gently laying her on the bed beside him.

"Where did that come from?" he asked her. She had never taken control of him like that before.

"I'm not quite sure," she answered. It wasn't like her at all to take control of a powerful man. But today, she felt the urge to do so.

* * *

After a brief nap, it was time to head back to Orlando. They had said their goodbyes to Claudia and Gracie felt saddened at leaving their new friend. But her mind was focused on the job they had to do. Tonight, the car ride went too quickly. They arrived at the exit to the alley, and Derek and Peter backed the trucks in.

They hoped no one would see their trucks in the alley, since the press conference blew their cover.

Jessie cupped Gracie's face in his hands. "I love

you," he said.

She smiled and kissed the inside of one of his palms. "I love you, too."

Landon opened the door and they waited while Clyde left the car in front of them to turn off power to the street. A few minutes later, there was a big blue explosion about four mansions down, and all the lights in the houses went black. Gracie ran from the car, not needing to take cover from the unpowered security cameras. As planned, Annie, Melissa, and Henry were at the gate.

"Step through the gate, we don't have much time. And hurry!" she yelled. The urgency in her voice had everyone running behind her to the trucks. Jessie, Landon, Luka, Gavin, Clyde, and Bubba got out, as she returned with her servants. "Get in and wait for me to get back. Do not get out!" Gracie ordered. "Annie, the press conference?" Gracie asked quickly.

"Lies! All Lies!"

Gracie nodded her head.

She turned once they were safely inside, and grabbed Jessie's hand. Everyone followed Gracie straight through the gate, and across the back property. They made it to the servants' quarters before Big Brother had made his way outside to cross the lawn and turn on the generator.

Gracie entered the door code and pulled it open. She remembered that the security doors stayed locked during a power outage. The keypads and locks were backed up by batteries. Once she entered the code, everyone piled inside. The servants had gathered in the living room to watch the nightly events. They couldn't help but stare at the menacing group of men with petite Gracie standing in the middle of them. She looked every bit as dangerous as they did. The group was monstrous. And there, leading them, was Gracie. Alive, as Melissa told them she would be.

The team followed her into the quarters, and then ran behind her toward doors that led into the kitchen. Only Gracie's flashlight was lit. The men seemed even more murderous in the dark shadows of her tiny light. The chefs were waiting for the power to come back on, but Gracie could feel their eyes follow them as they ran past the men toward the servants' stairs. She recognized many of them.

She had to look behind her more than once. As big as the guys were, they were very light on their feet. They didn't make a sound.

She couldn't get to Timmy's room fast enough. Once she was there she stopped for a moment and looked at Jessie. He nodded for her to go ahead, and she opened the door very slowly and quietly.

She tiptoed into his room. It looked exactly the same as when she lived there. Everything had been picked up off the floors; there wasn't a mess to be found in the five-year-old's bedroom. Rudy wouldn't have a mess in his house, even in a child's room. Then, she saw him, asleep in his bed. He had grown, and his hair was longer, brushing his eyelashes in his sleep. He looked sad. Gracie rushed over to his bed, but didn't wake him just yet. She bent down and found his packed bag under the foot of his bed. Melissa had done well.

She turned towards sleeping Timmy and brushed a hand over his forehead, removing his hair from his eyes. She gently shook him. At first, he just stirred in his sleep. She shook him a little harder and whispered in his ear, "Timmy, it's me. It's Gracie."

This time, he opened his eyes and sat up. She had the flashlight lying on the floor, but he could make out his older sister. "But you're dead," he said frightened and half asleep.

A tear fell from the corner of her eye. "No, baby,

I'm not. I'm right here, and I'm going to take you with me. Do you think you can be very quiet and come with me? I promise I will not ever leave you again!" she pleaded.

Timmy threw his arms around her, and she helped him out of bed. "Here, make sure you take your teddy and blankie," she said, opening up the bag to stuff them inside. "Let's get some shoes on you, too." Once that was done, she grabbed Timmy's hand and held on tight. She wasn't going to let go again. They reached the door and Timmy saw all the men standing on the other side. He was terrified.

"Gracie...!" he cried out.

"Shhhh. Timmy, it's ok! These are good guys. Rudy is a really bad guy now, and these good guys helped me get away from him. Now they're helping you get away from him. You can trust them," she whispered. He closed his eyes and clung to her arm. He was cutting off circulation, but she didn't care. She had her Timmy. As she passed the guys, she glanced back at Jessie and saw him entering Timmy's room. Then she lost sight of him. Turning her attention to the stairs, they quickly descended and were back in the kitchen within a few seconds. Timmy was running as fast as he could with her. They were making good time. Big Brother had still not turned on the generator.

Gracie and Timmy made it out of the servants' quarters and across the back yard, reaching the trucks in a matter of seconds. Once inside, she breathed for what felt like the first time. Annie and Melissa showered them with hugs. Henry ruffled the hair on Timmy's head as he clung to his sister.

Chapter Seventeen

The guys made it through Timmy's room, and cautiously made their way down the corridor of the second floor to the main staircase that would take them to the third floor, where Rudy's office was located. They knew Big Brother was on his way to the generator because they heard him leave the house. The only voices they heard were that of Rudy ordering Phillip to light candles in the office. They followed the voices.

"What's the matter with him?" Rudy asked impatiently. "I need to be able to see here!" He was obviously impatiently waiting for the generator to kick on. "Phillip, hurry up with those candles. I swear, if you didn't know so much already, I'd have you dead!" Rudy was about to get his wish, Jessie thought to himself.

"That's reassuring," Phillip said under his breath.

Jessie and the guys made it to the top of the stairs and were lined up on both sides of the French doors to Rudy's office. Just then, the lights turned back on. They knew they only had five minutes maximum to kill Rudy and Phillip and get off the property.

With a nod of his head, signaling the attack, Clyde and Bubba kicked opened the doors. Jessie, Landon, Gavin, and Luka flowed into the room with their guns drawn. Rudy was standing behind his desk, so startled by the intrusion that he fell backwards into his seat, rolling further away from his desk. Phillip shrieked like a little girl.

"Rudy," Jessie said. "We meet again!"

It took Rudy a moment to compose himself, but when he did, he stood up and took a few steps closer to his desk. Jessie knew there was a panic button underneath it. "Don't move one step closer or I'll kill you straight out," Jessie ordered.

Landon walked over to Phillip and made him hold onto the handle of his pistol. He put the gun in Phillip's hand and kept it there so Phillip's fingerprints would be the only person's on the gun. Jessie and his guys always wore their gloves. Landon placed Phillip's hand with the gun in it to his head. Phillip could be of no use to Rudy from that point forward.

"Now, is that any way to talk to the man who kept you safe and off the streets all these years?" Rudy asked in his cunning voice. "I suppose my wife's daughter is doing well?"

"She's none of your concern." Jessie walked farther into the room. Jessie walked over to Landon and Phillip and replaced his hand over Phillip's. Jessie made Phillip lift his arm and move the gun from pointing at his head to aim the gun precisely at Rudy's chest.

"Here's how this is going to go." Jessie took out a piece of paper with Rudy and Phillip's forged handwriting. It was an agreement of marriage between Phillip and Rudy concerning Gracie. "Phillip, you are going to walk over to Rudy." Jessie made him start walking closer. "You had an argument because Rudy just informed you that Gracie's dead. Phillip, you're enraged. You pull out this document here, guaranteeing your marriage to Gracie. Without her, you know you can't win this election. So you pull a gun and shoot Rudy square in the chest. One gunshot wound. If I was a more patient man, I'd make you suffer, but I've had enough of you myself," Jessie said, spitting his words at Rudy. He really couldn't stand the bastard.

Rudy just smiled. "Now Jessie, did you really think it would be that easy to kill me?"

Jessie smiled back, with his hand over Phillip's. "Yes, I do."

Jessie wasn't sure what had happened first. He saw movement out of the corner of his eye slide past the open doors, as sparks of gunshots moved along with it. Instantaneously, Jessie felt a heavy jolt and fire hit him in his left side, in the middle of his ribs. He cursed and in reaction, shot the gun he was forcing Phillip to hold. But Rudy was quick, even though he was an overly obese man. He had ducked behind the desk and pushed the panic button.

Landon screamed for Jessie to get down behind a chair, but adrenaline had kicked in. He held onto Phillip's hand even harder, forcing Phillip to move with him.

"Please!" Phillip pleaded. "I'm innocent in all of this! This was all Rudy's idea!"

"Was it Rudy's idea when you sexually assaulted my fiancé? Was it Rudy's idea when you backhanded her? Was it Rudy's idea to threaten to rape her?" Jessie screamed in Phillip's face. Phillip was shaking and Jessie had to hold on especially hard to keep Phillip's hand steady.

They circled around the desk, and found Rudy crouching under it. Rudy had pulled out his own gun and was waiting for them to turn the corner. Jessie pushed Phillip in front of him as a human shield. Rudy and Jessie fired at the same time. Phillip took the hit to the chest, just as Rudy took one to the head. Jessie let Phillip fall, then ducked behind the desk as another round of gunshots went flying past the door.

"It's gotta be the security officer!" Gavin yelled from behind a large chair. "There's only one of him, and all of us. I'm going out. Everyone follow close behind." He knew the direction of the last shots that were fired. They followed them. It was a good thing Gracie made them memorize all the passages to the house, because Gavin knew they could use another servants' staircase in the opposite direction to retreat if they had to.

Gavin fired as he rounded the doorframe and shot blindly in the direction of the staircase, building a human shield for the other guys.

"Go, now!" Gavin screamed.

* * *

Gracie and everyone in the cars knew that something went wrong. There were too many gunshots, too close together, then too far apart. "Stay here!" she yelled.

"Gracie, don't!" Derek yelled back at her, but she was already gone, through the gate and headed back to the house. Whoever was attacking the guys knew that they would not use the front entrance. He'd try to cut them off at the back door. Gracie went around to the side door of the attached servants' quarters, and crouched behind the bushes in the darkness, waiting.

Luka was closest to Jessie and helped him up and out of the room. They turned in the opposite direction, towards the back of the house, to retreat to the servants' stairs while the rest of the guys lined the hallway. Big Brother ran across the corridor from one room to the next. He and Gavin fired shots at each other without cover. Gavin felt a hit to the right arm and began retreating, trying to keep up with the rest of the guys. But he knew that Big Brother had to be killed, or he would give them away.

They turned left down another hallway and found the servants' staircase, leading directly to the servants' quarters. It was the servants' main stairwell that let out into the kitchen. They could then go through the servants' quarters and out the back door like they had come in. It was the perfect getaway. Once inside, they all paused to take inventory of their wounds. Three of them were shot: Jessie, Gavin, and Luka. Jessie's wound seemed to be the worst. He was losing a lot of blood. Luka ripped off his shirtsleeve and tied a tourniquet around his upper arm. Gavin realized he was just grazed on his calf by a bullet.

"You've gotta kill him," Jessie said holding his side. "I'll go back with you."

"No, you won't!" Luka said. They knew they had to get Jessie to a hospital, even if it risked their lives. "Landon, Gavin, and Bubba will stay behind. Clyde, I need your help getting Jessie across the lawn into the truck. We'll take off to the hospital. You guys call and we'll tell you where to go when you get back to the truck."

There was no time for another plan; they had to find Big Brother and kill him before the corrupted police officers got to the house. Luka started down the stairs with Jessie and Clyde. Gavin used the door to the stairwell as a shield as he peered around it. No one was in sight. They made their way through the third floor. Big Brother wasn't there. Then they proceeded to the second floor, down the main stairwell.

Outside, Gracie heard the sound of footsteps approaching the other side of the servants' quarters. She heard heavy breathing, but didn't recognize it. She peered around and saw a very scary looking man, trying to fit behind the shrubbery that she was so easily concealed in. He didn't see her. She was too well hidden. Covered by the darkness, she looked around the corner again, and saw him, crouched down, with two guns aimed at the back door. He was going to ambush the guys. Without much thinking, using the training she received in the mountains, she raised the gun at arm's length, aimed with both eyes open, and fired six rounds.

She watched each bullet hit the man and watched him hit the ground, blood seeping out from underneath him as he lay motionless, face down. Gracie had just killed her first person.

Hearing the gunshots coming from the yard, Gavin, Landon and Bubba raced down the remainder of the staircase, out the front door and around the side. Gracie was standing over the man's body with her gun pointed at him in case he might move. She wanted to be absolutely sure her guys got out of that house. She saw the three approaching, and then heard the back door open. Luka and Clyde were supporting Jessie, with a blood soaked sweatshirt.

"Oh my god," she said as she looked at his face. It was gray and covered in sweat.

They made their way across the back of the property, and reached the gates as they heard the first sounds of police cars in the distance. Cramming into the trucks, both Derek and Peter, with their lights off, made it out of the alleyway before the cops arrived. They had barely made it out alive and had left three dead bodies, a missing little boy, and three missing staff members behind.

"Go straight to the hospital," Luka ordered. Jessie tried to say something, but he lost consciousness. Gracie leaned over him trying to bring him back, but he had lost too much blood. Timmy was crying in the back seat.

When they arrived at the hospital, it took four guys to unload Jessie. Gracie stayed in the car with Annie, Melissa, Henry and Timmy. She knew if she was seen, they would relate Jessie's gunshot wound to the Talbot murder. The guys were really good at playing it off as an opposing gang encounter.

* * *

Not fully understanding the impact of the night's actions, Gracie cradled Timmy who eventually fell asleep in her arms. Melissa, who was about Gracie's age, put on some of Gracie's clothes, and went inside to relay messages back and forth from the guys to Gracie in the car. It took four hours for Jessie to get out of surgery. The bullet had grazed his ribcage, but he was going to be fine. He would have to stay in the hospital for a few days, but Luka, with his medical connections, had it arranged for Jessie to be transported to the hospital in St. Augustine for recovery. He explained that they were in the rival gang's territory, and it would safer for everyone, hospital staff included, if he were transported. The hospital put up no qualms about it.

Derek followed the ambulance to the hospital in St. Augustine. It was daybreak, and Gracie was running on pure adrenaline. Once they got Jessie settled into a room, Gracie disguised herself the best she could, and took the stairs to get to him. Luka kept watch and decided to stay with him until he was released. When Gracie entered, Luka sensed that she needed some alone time with Jessie, so he quietly stepped out of the room.

She walked over to the bed where Jessie was sleeping. She wasn't used to seeing him all hooked up to beeping machines. She was used to his big frame towering over her. In the hospital bed, he looked so fragile.

She kissed him, and then pulled a chair up next to the bed. "I killed my first person," she told him. He hadn't woken up yet, but Luka told her that he would be soon. He told her that talking to him might wake him sooner. "I knew he was going to ambush you, so I ran back. I waited for him to come around the side of the quarters, then I unloaded on him." She wasn't even looking at his face as she talked. She was too focused on all the machines he was hooked up to.

She was shocked to hear his voice. "Nice shot," he said weakly.

"Jessie!" she shrieked, standing up, leaning over his bed. He winced when she put the weight of her arm on his wound.

"Sorry! I'm so sorry! Are you in a lot of pain?" she asked him.

He was, but he wasn't going to admit it to her. "I'm fine," he said. Luka heard his voice and came back into the room. Gracie smiled her huge smile at him.

"Hey buddy! Had us all worried there for a while." Luka sat down on the other side of him. Jessie just nodded. He was exhausted.

"Gracie," he managed, "take care of Timmy for the next couple of days till I'm out of here. The guys will take care of me. You need to get out of here."

He was right, and now that he was awake and talking, Gracie felt more comfortable leaving him, although she never wanted to leave his side. She kissed him goodbye, kept her head low, and headed back out the way she came. When she met up with Derek, he drove her back to Claudia's B & B. Claudia was surprised to see them, but had kept their rooms available for another night just in case. She had a knack for knowing what they needed. Derek and Clyde explained everything to her while Gracie took

Timmy into her room. He hadn't spoken since they left the mansion.

She sat him down in a chair, and then sat on the floor in front of him, as she had always done when they were having a serious conversation. She liked to be on his level. "Timmy, are you ok?" she asked him.

He just stared at her and started to cry. "He told me you were dead and mama didn't want me anymore!" Gracie started to cry as well. He flew off the chair and wrapped his arms around her. Apparently, he only felt comfortable if some part of him was clinging onto her.

"Let me tell you what happened, ok?" He drew his head back and wiped his runny nose with the back of his hand. She smiled at the familiar gesture. "You remember the night I was taken away by the scary men at the ice cream shop?" He nodded. "Well, was I in for a surprise!" she said trying to make the story sound like a grand fairy tale. She must have succeeded, because when Claudia knocked on the door to let them know breakfast was ready, Timmy was rambling through the whole story, embellishing the parts he thought were the best.

When they got to the breakfast table, Timmy had turned back into his talkative, five-year-old self.

"Hi!" he said to the guys, minus Luka and Jessie who were still at the hospital. He sat between Gracie and Melissa. "This is my sister Gracie, and she killed a whole bunch of crazy mean men to save me!" he exclaimed. They all smiled and some laughed.

"Yes, apparently, there's more than one now!" Gracie said with a chuckle. Timmy ran through the whole story again, oblivious to the fact that these guys knew and were a part of the whole thing. But it warmed her heart to see them act so engrossed in his story they let their breakfast go cold just to listen to him.

After breakfast, Melissa and Annie took Timmy back to his room. Gracie and the guys needed to figure out what they were going to do.

"It's all over the news. Rudy Talbot, his closest accomplice, and their bodyguard are dead," Clyde filled them all in.

"Thank God!" Gracie exclaimed. "Who do they think did it?"

Clyde smiled. "Well, apparently a deal went wrong between Rudy and Phillip over you, Gracie. An argument ensued. They shot and killed each other. But the bodyguard.... apparently a neighbor saw a woman shoot him. They have no idea who she is, but are speculating that she might be one of the missing servants." Clyde waited for a moment as Gracie smiled. "I wonder who that woman might be?"

"I have no idea!" Gracie said laughing.

"I almost killed you myself when you left the truck," Derek said under his breath, clearly not as enthused as the rest of the guys. "You could have gotten killed."

"Instead, she unloaded six rounds into the son of a bitch," Bubba said laughing hysterically. "Congrats, Gracie ma'am! You made your first hit!"

She just shook her head. She knew she killed a man, but she didn't feel the least bit guilty about it. Probably because he had shot her Jessie. "Gee, thanks guys," she said sarcastically. "So what now?"

"Let's just enjoy St. Augustine for a few days. Then we'll head back home when Jessie's released in a few days."

Gracie just shook her head. She couldn't believe she was casually having a conversation about hit teams and killing men at the breakfast table. But she was going to do just as Jessie had said and enjoy her time with Timmy.

Chapter Eighteen

They spent the next few days lounging around Claudia's. Their pictures were all over the news: the five gunmen who abducted Gracie months ago, the missing servants, Gracie, and Timmy. They needed to keep a low profile until they could get to the Poconos.

Annie had turned back into the motherly figure Gracie had missed so much during the past few years. And Melissa had quickly become her best friend. It also didn't escape her that Gavin seemed to take a liking to Melissa and she to him. They sat together at the dinner table, stayed up late on the front porch talking, and she blushed whenever he looked her way.

"You know, he's a good guy," Gracie said as they sat on the front porch swing, watching Timmy chase lizards in the garden in the courtyard of the B & B.

Melissa blushed. "I know," she said. "I just never pictured myself with anyone. I always accepted my status as a servant for rich people. I was ok with that."

"I was too," Annie added. "But I'd much rather be with you guys in that wonderful mountain cabin you can't stop raving about."

"Well these guys mean business. All the time. So if Gavin's got his sights on you, which he does, and you seem to be interested, which you do, I'd suggest

you start thinking of yourself a little bit differently!"
Gracie added.

"I guess I better," she said under her breath. The
three women started laughing.

They headed back inside, so Gracie could go visit
Jessie. It had only been a week and a half since they
arrived back in Florida. For Gracie, that was long
enough. But she had one more matter of business
she needed to finish before they left Florida for good.

* * *

With a few days to go until Jessie was released from
the hospital, Gracie had some business to take care
of. She needed Peter and Bubba to escort her to
Orlando. Her first stop was to the police station.
Mouths dropped wide open when she walked in.

"I need to speak with Chief Brunnell," Gracie said
coolly, yet confidently.

She didn't see him walk up behind her. "Where
the hell have you been?"

When she turned around, he gawked at her
pregnant stomach.

"I ran away. Rudy wanted me to marry Phillip and
I was in love with someone else. We didn't have
cable. I had no idea what was going on until I read
the paper yesterday." Gracie was a very convincing
liar. "I just came here to tell you that I'm alive.
Apparently, Rudy's press conference about Timmy
was a lie because he's fine. I was able to retrieve him
from relatives this morning."

"Well, I'll be damned." Chief Brunnell said.

"If you need anything else from me, you can speak
with my lawyer." Gracie turned and walked out.
Peter and Bubba had stayed in the car since their
pictures were plastered all around the station.

They let her go without bothering to question her.

Even the Chief of Police seemed to breathe a bit easier with Rudy out of the picture. And since Gracie gained nothing financially from the deaths of Rudy and Phillip, she wasn't seen as a suspect.

Her next stop was to her attorney's office. Gracie's lawyer was especially curious what she was up to. He didn't raise any red flags with authorities, she just peaked his personal interest.

"Why do you want your mother to sign over custody of Timmy to you?" Mr. Dower asked her. "Because of her mental health?" he probed.

"Something like that," Gracie said, staying vague as possible, while still getting the proper documentation she needed.

"Because she's in the mental institution, you'll need to get a doctor to sign here," Mr. Dower pointed to the spot, "to show that your mother is not competent enough to make such a decision." Mr. Dower pointed to another page, "And, as Timothy's next blood relative, custody will automatically go to you."

Gracie nodded that she understood.

"You're also petitioning for Mr. Talbot's inheritance to go to your mother instead of Timmy?" Mr. Dower asked her.

"That's correct," she said. Rudy left everything to his sole heir, Timmy. But gaining custody of Timmy meant that Gracie made decisions for him, not their mother. This would ensure that her mother could live a very fulfilling life in the mental institution, never having to worry about money. And never having to bother Gracie or Timmy again.

"I must confess I do not understand why you don't want any inheritance to go to Timmy. Honestly, the two of you would be set for life." Mr. Dower tried to gain some understanding of what Gracie was thinking.

"I'm sorry you don't understand" was all Gracie was willing to give up.

"Since your mother cannot make any decisions at the moment, you need to decide what you want to do about the mansion and Blanchen Hotels," Mr. Dower went on, pulling out a few more papers from his stack.

"I'm sorry?" Gracie said, confused. "What do you mean about Blanchen Hotels?"

Mr. Dower took off his glasses. "After your father died, your mother inherited the hotels. But he stipulated in his will that if she were ever unable to fulfill her role as executor of the hotels, the role would go to you. As far as I know, Rudy had run them since your mother married him. But now, with Rudy dead and your mother's mental health being as it is, the executor position will go to you, if you accept it."

Gracie just stared at her attorney. She had no idea she would inherit her father's hotel chain. "Put the mansion up for auction as soon as possible. I will accept the executor position of Blanchen Hotels." Gracie signed a few papers for both issues.

"Get the paperwork filled out concerning Timmy and just return it to my office. We'll take care of everything else. Is there a number I can reach you at?" he asked.

"I'll be in touch," Gracie said, getting up out of the chair. "Mr. Dower," she hesitated, as she was about to walk out of the door. "Thank you for everything you've done for me over the years." She knew she'd never see the man again.

She guessed that he knew the same. "You're welcome, Miss Gracie. Best of luck to you and your baby."

"Thank you," and with that, she turned and walked out.

* * *

Gracie waited until the day before they left Orlando to visit her mother. Once again, Peter and Bubba accompanied Gracie. She swore that if she ever saw Orlando again, it would be too soon. She didn't trust that her mother wouldn't enlist the help of some of Rudy's old friends to find Gracie. She wasn't exactly sure what her mother thought of Rudy – whether she was under his control or whether she actually loved him and honored him. So she played her cards safe. She didn't want anything stopping her from gaining sole physical custody of Timmy.

They drove to The Brywn Mental Institution of Orlando. It was located one block down from the hospital Jessie was taken to after the shooting.

Gracie didn't know if her mother had seen any of the news conferences or if she still thought Gracie was dead. And Gracie didn't know what state of mind she would find her mother in. Did she really break down? Or was it all a charade like Gracie had thought? She'd find out soon enough.

Gracie did nothing to hide her appearance. With Peter on one side and Bubba on the other, she walked into the lobby of the institution carrying a mound of paper work.

"I'm here to see Patty Talbot," Gracie said calmly.

The receptionist must have recognized her from TV. "I'm sure your mother will be glad you're back! She hasn't had a visitor since she entered," the receptionist told her.

Gracie just nodded. She wasn't sure what to say to that.

"Before I see my mother, I need to talk privately with her main physician," Gracie added.

The receptionist nodded, and picked up the phone on her desk. "Paging Dr. Brown. Paging Dr. Brown. Please call the front reception desk." She put the phone down and then motioned toward the sitting room. "Why don't the three of you sit down and wait for Dr. Brown to take you back. He should only be a moment."

Gracie smiled at the woman and thanked her for her help. The three of them sat down and waited. A few minutes later, an older gentleman with gray hair wearing a white jacket over his designer suit came out of the security-coded double doors.

"Ms. Talbot," he said extending his hand as Gracie stood up.

"It's Ms. Conners," Gracie corrected. She decided that since they were engaged she could start to use Jessie's last name. Besides, she wanted to rid herself of everything that had to do with Rudy. "This is Peter and Bubba. They are my family members."

Dr. Brown nodded. "I see," he said.

"I'd like to talk with you privately before seeing my mother," she told him.

Dr. Brown motioned toward the doors, but walked in front of them, typing in the pass code that opened them. "Let's go to my office," he said as he led them back into the doctors' wing of the institution.

Once inside Dr. Brown's office, Gracie sat down across the desk from him. Peter took one chair, but Bubba stayed by the door. Dr. Brown believed that Peter was family, but knew Bubba was Gracie's security guard. He knew Rudy Talbot more than he wanted to and didn't blame Gracie one bit for being cautious even after the man was pronounced dead. Gracie saw the large, open file with her mother's picture in it on his desk.

"What can I do for you?" Dr. Brown asked her.

"Tell me about my mother," she said emotionless.

He took a deep breath and sat forward, folding his hands together. "Gracie, your mother had been under the influence of a very manipulative man for your entire life. He's brainwashed her to believe so many things; the state of her mental health is questionable. I don't believe she has a mental disorder. But I do believe she will need years of therapy," Dr. Brown told her.

Gracie nodded. "So what you're telling me is that she has no known mental illness, but is not sound enough to make her own decisions."

"Precisely. When you were abducted, Rudy told everyone close to him that you were killed. Your mother did have a mental breakdown. She did need to be in here. However, after she had been in therapy for a little while and treated with medication, she could have gone home to get on with her life. But Rudy never checked her out. He called me a few times to check on her to make sure she stayed in here, but that was it. You're her first visitor." Dr. Brown let the weight of that settle in with Gracie.

Gracie set the stack of papers on his desk. "Do you believe she is capable of raising a five-year-old?" she asked.

"No, not at this time."

"I need you to sign these papers signing custody of my younger brother over to me." She motioned toward one stack of papers, and the "sign here" tab her lawyer had provided. "Then, I need you to sign for her on this page, saying she is not capable of making her own decisions."

Dr. Brown nodded and signed the papers immediately without hesitation.

"I'd like to see my mother now," she said.

Gracie's heart was beating out of her chest. She felt so many different emotions. She was sad she hadn't had the mother she always wanted growing up. She was angry for everything her mother put her through just being married to Rudy. She hated her for all those years of loyalty to Rudy when she should have been loyal to her daughter. But when she rounded the hall corner opening into a sitting room with white walls, floors, and furniture and patients in white pants and tops, she felt pity for her mother.

She sat at a small table in front of a window staring outside with a blank expression on her face. Gracie stopped a second and took a breath. Peter and Bubba were right behind her, but understood she needed to do this alone.

"We'll wait right here," Bubba said.

Dr. Brown accompanied Gracie over to her mother. "Mrs. Talbot," he said gently, touching her shoulder.

She jerked, as if she was lost in thoughts far away from reality. When she turned around, she saw Gracie. They stared at each other for what seemed like eternity. Then Gracie sat down in the other chair at the table and grabbed her mother's hand. It was cold and skinny to the bone. Not what she remembered of her mother.

"Mother, it's me, Gracie." She said. "I'm alive."

Her mother burst into tears. "Gracie!" she cried. "Rudy told me you were dead!"

Gracie tried hard to keep her emotions in check, but a small tear escaped her eye. It wasn't a tear of a joyful reunion or a tear of sadness from not seeing her mother for so long. It was a tear for all the pain Rudy had ruthlessly put her through. It was a tear for the woman who resembled her mother, but had become far from that which Gracie longed for.

Gracie didn't say anything. She just held her mother's hand. "Rudy's dead, Gracie. Phillip killed him because of you! Why couldn't you cooperate just this once? Phillip was a good man! And now look at you, sleeping around getting yourself knocked up! Rudy was so right about you! You are a little slut!"

Gracie now understood what Dr. Brown had meant by years of brainwashing.

"I know he's dead, Mom. Aren't you worried about Timmy?" Gracie questioned, trying to keep her anger in check. Her mother was obviously grieving over the death of her belated husband. Gracie just couldn't fathom why anyone would grieve over the loss of Rudy Talbot.

Patty nodded but said nothing.

That was all it took for the ice to cover Gracie's face. "Mother, the Doctor signed papers saying that you cannot make decisions. That means I am now the legal guardian of Timmy."

Patty wiped at her tears as she absorbed what Gracie was saying. "Gracie Ann Talbot!" she exclaimed. "Your father is dead and now you're trying to take my son away from me? Where is your sense of compassion?"

"Mother, Rudy is not my father. Rudy killed my father, and if you weren't so brainwashed by him, you'd have seen that." Gracie was tired of games. Rudy had created a guilt-tripping woman, and Gracie wasn't going to put up with one more of Rudy's games.

"Gracie!" her mother said in disbelief and pulled her hands away from her daughter's. "How can you be so insensitive?" she demanded.

Gracie's face was emotionless. She no longer felt anything for the woman that was sitting at the table. Not even pity. It wasn't her mother. Gracie realized her mother had died long ago. This woman was a product of Rudy Talbot, years in the making.

Patty sat back in her chair and gasped at her daughter. "Rudy was right about you. You're an ungrateful little brat." Gracie stood up and pushed back from the table. Dr. Brown had stayed in the room, unsure of what would happen. Gracie nodded at him, and he back at her, Patty began to yell, then scream at her daughter.

"You little brat! You whore! How could you do this to me?" Patty screamed.

"Mrs. Talbot, please calm down or we'll have to medicate you," Dr. Brown said loudly over the screams as two nurses and another doctor ran into the sitting room.

"You need to medicate that pregnant tramp! She stole my son! She's the reason my husband is dead. He was a good man!" Patty would never be able to see the truth. Maybe that's why it was so easy for Gracie to walk away without looking back.

Dr. Brown nodded at them, as the other doctors and nurses tried to contain Patty.

Gracie followed Dr. Brown back to the doors they had entered through, and then walked out of the institution with Peter and Bubba behind her.

Once back in the truck, Gracie sighed and rubbed her eyes with her hands.

"Are you alright Ms. Gracie?" Bubba asked.

"I will be," she answered as she looked up at him.

On the way back to St. Augustine, Gracie dropped off the papers to her attorney's office. Timmy was now hers. Patty would be spending the rest of her life in The Brywn Mental Institution. Rudy's inheritance and life insurance would pay the costs of Patty's mental healthcare. The mansion, with everything in it, would go up for auction next month. Gracie made sure to legally wash her hands of any material possession belonging to her past, with the exception of the hotels. She had plans for them.

* * *

When they got back to St. Augustine, Gracie sent Peter to see Jessie. She was too tired and knew he'd understand. Annie and Melissa were watching Timmy, and she decided she needed a hot bath after that trip.

Gracie thought of the past week-and-a-half in Orlando. Before they came down, she was without Jessie for three months. During the course of the past two weeks, he had been shot, and almost died and spent the majority of it in the hospital recuperating. Gracie planned to have a very heavily-worded talk with Jessie about being away from her when they got back to the mountains.

She couldn't believe they were headed back to the mountains tomorrow. It was late March, and the last of the snowstorms should be passing through. She'd finally get to experience her first spring in the Poconos. And she'd get to go out and see the town. But the first thing she planned on doing was going to see a doctor about her baby. She hadn't had any prenatal care and wanted to know that everything was ok before she went into labor.

That night, she packed up all of her, Jessie's, and Timmy's belongings. Afterwards, she sat in the kitchen with Claudia for over an hour, thanking her for all her help and talking of the future. Claudia had plans to open up another B & B next door to the Inn on Charlotte. Gracie told her all about their cabin up north, and Claudia promised to come visit. Gracie even tried to convince Claudia to open up a B & B in the Poconos.

When she walked out of the kitchen, Landon was waiting for her.

"Is everything ok?" she asked yawning.

"Oh yeah," he said, quickly putting her at ease. "We just got back from our house in Orlando. Picked up some of our belongings before heading up north tomorrow with you guys."

"I'm glad you will be coming along. Nothing like having family around," she said with a smile.

Landon gave her a hug before she retired into her room. She slept soundly that night, dreaming of Brear and Honey. Of the snow on the mountains, and the cute little room off the loft with the picturesque view.

Chapter Nineteen

Jessie was released the next morning. He was a strong man, and was healing quickly. They made him comfortable in the truck and headed up I-95 toward their Pocono cabin. Timmy rode with Gracie and Jessie, along with Derek, Clyde, Luka, and Annie. Melissa opted to ride with Gavin, Landon, Peter, and Bubba. The trip took another sixteen hours, but when they finally made it back, Gracie noticed that most of the snow had melted. It looked like they were in for an early spring. They approached the gate, entered the property and turned the corner toward the cabin. It looked even more beautiful than she had remembered.

"Wow!" Timmy exclaimed. Gracie and Jessie smiled at each other. Timmy and Jessie had instantly taken a liking to each other and bonded within the first hour in the truck. Gracie and everyone else in the Tahoe were subjected to hours of what sounded like father-son bantering back and forth about whether Mario Brothers or Sonic the Hedge Hog was the coolest old school game.

Seeing Timmy's reaction, she knew they were going to be happy here. Hearing the cars pull up, Brear and Honey came barreling out of the dog door.

"Cool!" Timmy yelled. "I have dogs!" Gracie knew she was home.

Everyone piled out of the trucks, stretching, and

grabbing an arm full of bags to take inside. Clyde and Luka helped Jessie upstairs to the bedroom and got him situated. Gracie told Timmy to wait downstairs while she followed them.

"Well this is certainly a turn-around from last October when I was laid up in bed," Gracie joked as she snuggled into Jessie's good side.

He laughed. "Yeah, but I recover faster than you do," he said, wrapping his arm tight around her. "It's good to be home," he said looking around their cozy cabin room.

"Yes it is!" she said. They could hear Timmy's youthful laughter and the dogs barking, and they smiled at each other. But they were the only two in their room, and that's all that mattered to Gracie.

He smiled and pulled her close. He kissed her, forgetting about his gunshot wound and sore side. They were going to be a family: he, Gracie, Timmy, the baby, and the rest of the gang. And they were going to be safe, and able to live their lives in the mountains thanks in large part to Gracie.

* * *

It took Jessie all of one week to get annoyed with bed-rest and to start moving around the cabin again. He insisted on going to Gracie's doctor appointment with her. Peter drove them, but stayed in the car. Melissa and Gavin offered to watch Timmy.

"I still don't understand why you're putting yourself through pain to go to a doctor's appointment. It's not like the baby's being born," Gracie said to him.

"I'm only a first-time dad once. I don't want to miss any more than I already have," he said.

Dr. Shaw was the town's only obstetrics doctor. He was in his mid-fifties and had a warm and

welcoming smile. He didn't make Gracie feel bad for
not having any prenatal care for the first five, now
almost six months, of her pregnancy. But just to
make sure everything was ok, Dr. Shaw ordered a
whole panel of tests on her. They checked her urine,
took three vials of blood, listened to the heartbeat,
measured her stomach, and then took her to the
ultrasound room.

"Is everything alright?" she asked as they sprayed
cold gel on her stomach.

"Seems to be. Most women get ultrasounds at
twenty weeks to see what they're having. So this is
routine. But you are measuring big for six months,
so we want to make sure your due date is correct."

Gracie looked at Jessie. "It has to be. We've only
been together for six months and I wasn't with
anyone before that. Ever," she said.

Jessie held her hand as they started the
ultrasound. "Do you want to know what you're
having?" Dr. Shaw asked with a smile on his face.

She looked at Jessie. "Yes!" he exclaimed before
she could answer.

He pointed to the screen. "You see this here?" he
asked.

Jessie and Gracie nodded.

"That's baby number one," Dr. Shaw said. "This
right here is baby number two. Congratulations!
You're having twins!"

"What?" Gracie asked in shock. She couldn't take
her eyes off the image on the ultrasound machine.
Two little bodies next to each other, inside her.

"Are you sure?" Jessie asked.

Dr. Shaw just laughed. "Yes! You are definitely
having twins! Now let's see if we can find out the sex
of them." It seemed like hours. Dr. Shaw was moving
the ultrasound wand around on her stomach and
was hitting a button that took pictures and then

printed them out for Gracie and Jessie to take home. She could have spent the rest of her life looking at her babies on that machine.

"Alright," Dr. Shaw finally said. "Baby one, which we'll call Baby A, is a boy."

Gracie smiled and looked at Jessie. He was grinning from ear to ear.

After another few minutes that seemed like eternity, Dr. Shaw announced that Baby B was a girl. Gracie looked back to Jessie, but this time his face was white.

"What's wrong?" she asked.

"I don't know what to do with a little girl," Jessie admitted. "Boys I can handle. A little girl, she's not dating until she's thirty! Wait, never! She's never dating!" he exclaimed.

Gracie and Dr. Shaw laughed. "Well you'll get to ground her for life from boys soon enough. Twins usually deliver a month early. So you've got about two more months max. Your cervix is already thinning out, so I want you off your feet. You don't have to be on bed rest, but I want you resting." Dr. Shaw went over everything else Gracie needed to know before going into labor, and what to look for as signs of labor. She hoped to have them naturally, and as long as they stayed head down, the doctor explained, she'd be able to. But if they turned, she'd have to have a C-section.

They left Dr. Shaw's office two hours later. Peter was starting to worry, and got more worried as he saw the look on Jessie's face when they walked out of the building.

"What's wrong, Boss?" Peter asked.

"It's a little girl!" he said.

"And a little boy!" Gracie exclaimed. "We're having twins!"

"Holy shit!" Peter shouted! "That's awesome!" Then

he started laughing. "And one's a girl! Serves you right, Boss!" Gracie couldn't help but laugh as well.

Once they got back to the house, everyone was waiting in the living room to hear the news. They all stayed silent for just a moment as they took in the news that Gracie was having twins. Then congratulatory hugs and handshakes were all around and Gracie was showing everyone the ultrasound images Dr. Shaw let her take home.

"Well, what are they?" Melissa asked.

Peter just started laughing. "Man, Karma's a bitch!"

Jessie punched him in the arm. "One girl and one boy." Everyone got excited all over again. Especially Timmy. "I'm gonna be a big brother!" he shouted over and over jumping on the couch. Gracie didn't miss the little wink that Gavin sent Melissa's way when she smiled at him from across the room. They would be next, she thought to herself.

The rest of the night everyone spent gathered in the cabin's living room, eating hamburgers and talking baby. Since they didn't have any friends in their new home to invite to a baby shower, Annie and Melissa promised to decorate the nursery, which was going to be the room off the loft. Gracie was thankful for the help, especially since she was supposed to be resting

Jessie just kept shaking his head in disbelief every time he thought about it. He was tired from the day, and a little sore, but he didn't let it show. He needed to be ok for Gracie now.

* * *

The next few weeks were a whirlwind. Annie and Melissa made good on their promise and decorated the nursery in baby blue with a polka dot theme.

Blue was her and Jessie's favorite color, and the polka dots made it girlie enough for their daughter. Timmy helped, of course. He was glued to Gracie's side. Everyone was bonding with Timmy, especially Jessie.

"How come I don't have my own room?" Timmy asked. "I'm the big brother. I have to have someplace to go when they babies are crying!"

Gracie laughed. Timmy hadn't wanted his own room. He had been sleeping on the floor in Gracie's bedroom. Jessie didn't mind, although he was ready for Timmy to feel comfortable enough to sleep in his own room. But even if Timmy was in his own room, Gracie's baby belly made making love impossible.

They were sitting downstairs with everyone. Gavin was the first to break the silence. "Well, Boss, we were all talking last night. With the babies coming any time now, we're afraid we're crowding the house. We've all picked a spot of land to build our own cabins, but it's going to take a little while to get them done. We were thinking that Annie could stay here and help with the babies and Timmy. But the rest of us, well, we thought that we could stay at the lodge in town for a few months until our cabins are built."

"No!" Gracie exclaimed. "You're family. Family stays together." She did not like the idea of her guys having to stay in a hotel until their cabins were built. It was spring, and they had already broken ground on several of them.

"Gracie, you're not going to want all of us here. And you guys need to bond as a family. It won't be for long. We have to get the cabins finished before the first snowfall. And we'll be here all the time anyway!" Melissa chimed in.

Jessie looked around at his guys, and then at Gracie. He was ready to just be with her and Timmy. Funny now how the thought of Gracie was never without the thought of Timmy. "As long as you all promise to still be here all the time," Jessie said.

And they did. No one left until the end of the week. Gracie only had two more weeks left, maximum. Jessie didn't know how her stomach could keep growing. It seemed like those babies were going to break out if Gracie didn't push them out soon. She was exhausted and slept a lot that week.

Their first night alone together was a Friday night. Melissa and Annie had made them dinner. Spaghetti with meatballs, one of Gracie's favorites. Timmy led the conversation at dinner, as usual, and busted into giggling fits between stories. Jessie laughed with him, and pretty soon, it was clear that Jessie and Timmy were up to something.

"What's going on with you two?" she asked, laughing at them.

"We have a surprise for you!" Timmy exclaimed. "It's really for me, but it's for you too. But it's really mine."

Jessie laughed. "Don't give it away!"

They were finished eating and Jessie asked if they should show her. Timmy shot out of his chair like a torpedo and grabbed Gracie's hand. It took her a second to get up, but then she followed Timmy down the hallway past the kitchen where the bedrooms were on the ground floor. Jessie was right behind them. They stopped at the first bedroom on the right, located between the kitchen and the downstairs bathroom. The door was closed, and Gracie didn't understand why they were standing in the hallway.

Timmy couldn't stop giggling. "Well," Jessie finally said. "Are you going to open the door, Goofball?"

"Close your eyes!" Timmy ordered.

Gracie smiled and did as she was told. "Just don't ask me to walk anywhere with my eyes closed." She heard the door open and Timmy run inside and jump on the bed.

"Open!" he screamed as loud as he could.

When Gracie opened her eyes, she couldn't believe what she saw. The room was painted a bright boyish blue. There was a border going around the center of the room with dinosaurs all over it. The comforter on the twin bed was dinosaurs and there were pictures of dinosaurs on the walls. It was a five-year-old's dream room. His name was hung up above his bed in white painted letters.

Jessie wrapped his arms around Gracie. "Do you like it?"

She wiped a tear away from her eye. "When did you do this?"

"We've been working on it for a little while," Jessie admitted a little sheepishly. He hated keeping things from her, but he knew how much this would mean to her.

Timmy kept jumping on his bed. "The day you found out about the babies, Jessie asked me what kind of room I wanted! He said it wasn't fair the babies got a special room and I didn't! So I picked dinosaurs! And then Melissa and Annie took me shopping for clothes! I have a whole new robe!" he exclaimed.

Gracie walked into the room and started opening the drawers to his dresser. He was right. He had a whole new "robe," as Timmy called it. His drawers were organized, and so was his closet. He not only had new clothes, but new toys as well. She couldn't stop herself from crying.

Hugging Jessie, she wiped at her tears. "Thank you," she said quietly.

"You're welcome," he whispered back. "So does this mean that you're going to sleep in here?"

"Yup! But if I have a nightmare, can I sleep with you?" Timmy asked, still jumping on his bed.

"You betcha!" Jessie said.

"Look Gracie! Jessie said I could have a walkie-talkie like the babies!" He pointed towards the monitor on the nightstand, next to a light-up dinosaur nightlight that changed colors.

"I know you wouldn't feel comfortable with Timmy staying on the ground floor unless you could hear him, so I told him about the walkie-talkies, and if he ever had a nightmare, all he has to do is talk into it, and we'll come get him to sleep with us," Jessie said.

Now Gracie really couldn't stop crying. Not only had he made Timmy a part of the family, but he thought out what would make both Timmy and her feel better.

They spent two hours looking at everything in Timmy's room. Then, Gracie sent him to the bathroom for his nighttime bath. She laughed as she heard Jessie and Timmy making dinosaur noises from the bathroom as she searched Timmy's drawers to find his pajamas. Sure enough, every single pair had dinosaurs on them.

When she stood up, she felt a sharp pain in her lower stomach. She clutched onto the bureau and took a few deep breaths. Then it went away. Braxton Hicks, she thought to herself, and went about turning down Timmy's bed for the night. She made sure the night-light was plugged in and the baby monitor, or walkie- talkie as Jessie called it, was turned on. In bed with him, were his comfort items from the mansion. She was glad she had thought to bring them. As she stood up straight again from turning on the baby monitor, she felt another sharp pain. This one included not only her lower stomach, but also her sides. She sat down on the edge of the bed and took another few deep breaths.

Timmy ran into the room wrapped in a towel. Gracie threw his underwear at him and he giggled like the happiest little boy while he got dressed.

"Are you ok?" Jessie asked. Gracie looked a little pale and tired.

"Umm-hmmm," she said as she rubbed her stomach. She sat on the edge of the bed to read Timmy a nighttime story. Then stood up, and got another sharp pain. This time, it had her bending over in pain.

"What's wrong?" Jessie asked.

"I don't know! Whenever I stand up, I start getting really sharp pains in my stomach," she said. She was scared. It wasn't like the contractions Dr. Shaw had warned her about. It was only when she stood up. She didn't understand it.

"Are you ok, Gracie?" Timmy asked.

"Oh yeah!" she lied. "Just a stomach ache from laughing so hard! Sleep good baby! I love you!" She gave him a kiss and walked out of the room as the pain started to let up again.

"Love you, man!" Jessie said from the door.

"Love you guys, too!" Timmy yelled as Jessie left the door cracked about an inch.

Chapter Twenty

Gracie took two steps towards the living room, and then grabbed the wall as another pain covered her entire stomach and lower back. It was all she could do to stay standing. Jessie put his arms around her to help support her.

"I think I'm in labor," she said between deep breaths. "Call Melissa and Gavin." They had a labor plan. And Melissa and Gavin would stay with Timmy until Gracie and Jessie were back from the hospital. Jessie helped Gracie to the couch, and then picked up his cell phone and called them. Gracie had another contraction and had to lie down on the couch to keep from getting dizzy. They were breathtakingly painful, not at all what she expected. She had expected the pain to slowly increase, not knock her off her feet.

Melissa and Gavin drove one of the trucks up to the house, the one with the car seats already installed. Melissa rushed inside to Gracie while Jessie ran upstairs to get her bags.

"We didn't tell Timmy anything," she told Melissa. "We'll call you as soon as the babies are here!"

Jessie had to wait out a contraction before Gracie was able to get up and walk to the car. The ride to the hospital was painful. She felt too much pressure on her pelvic bone, she thought it was going to break with every little bump they hit on the road. Once they arrived at the hospital, they put Gracie in a wheelchair and wheeled her up to the maternity ward. Jessie parked the car, and then joined her. She was already in a gown and hooked up to monitors by the time he got there. They were doing an ultrasound on her to check the position of the babies.

But Jessie could tell when he walked in, something wasn't right. Gracie was in extreme pain, and there were multiple doctors and nurses bustling around. "Jessie!" she cried out. He went over to her to hold her hand.

"Gracie, one of the babies has changed positions, which is why your labor started so quickly and so intensely. We're going to have to perform an emergency C-section. The baby that has moved is sitting on the other baby's umbilical cord." Dr. Shaw quickly walked out of the room while the nurses went about preparing Gracie for surgery.

"What's going on?" she asked Jessie. She was scared. More scared than she'd been the night she was abducted. More scared than she was the night they took Timmy and she killed her first person. Those nights, her adrenaline raced through her veins. Tonight, though, she felt pure terror.

"I don't know," Jessie said watching the nurses. Two of them got behind the bed and started to push Gracie out of the room. Jessie stayed by her side until they told him he couldn't go any farther.

"Wait!" Gracie yelled.

"Ma'am, we have to get you into surgery!" the nurse exclaimed.

She looked at Jessie. "Whatever happens, make sure the babies are ok!" They wheeled her off. It was the last thing she said to Jessie before they took her away from him.

Another nurse gently took Jessie by the arm. "Is

there anyone I can call to come be with you? This surgery is going to take a little while. But as soon as the babies are born and are ok, you can be with them in the nursery until your wife is out of surgery."

Everything was moving in slow motion. "Yeah," he said, as he wrote down Gavin's phone number for the nurse to call. He knew Melissa and Gavin would get word to everyone. And they did.

Within twenty minutes, the waiting room was packed with everyone besides Melissa, Gavin, and Timmy. Jessie sat in a chair with his head in his hands. He had put Gracie in one dangerous situation after another. He was cursing himself and the choices he made concerning the woman he loved. He decided that he should have just taken her the moment he fell in love with her five years ago. He shouldn't have waited for Rudy to try to kill her four times. He should have known more about her. Then she wouldn't have almost died from her asthma attack. He should have worn protection. What did he think was going to happen if they had sex everyday without it? He shouldn't have let her near Rudy again the night of the murder. She and their babies could have been killed by that security guard. And now she was in emergency surgery, her life and the babies at risk again.

"Jessie, you can't beat yourself up about this. Twins are complicated," Landon said, but Jessie didn't want to hear it.

"Every decision I've made has been selfish and Gracie should have never been in this situation to begin with! Maybe if she had gotten prenatal care, or things hadn't been so stressful during her pregnancy...," he trailed off when he saw Dr. Shaw and a nurse walking down the hallway. Everyone in the waiting room stood up. Jessie's face went white.

"Mr. Conners, we did the emergency surgery and both babies are doing fine and are in the nursery. They received nines on the Apgar Scale. They couldn't be healthier." He breathed a sigh of relief, and then realized Dr. Shaw hadn't commented on Gracie.

"Is she ok?" he whispered.

"We had some complications getting the babies out. We had to make the incision larger than normal. And because it took us longer to get both babies out, there was a lot of bleeding. She's in the intensive care unit getting a blood transfusion. She hasn't woken up yet."

Landon put a hand on Jessie's shoulder. "What does that mean?" Landon asked for Jessie.

"It means she lost a lot of blood. She's getting more now, but we don't know if there are any long term effects."

Landon still spoke for Jessie. "What kind of long term effects?"

"It's too early to know. Why don't I take you back to the nursery to see the babies?" Dr. Shaw said.

Jessie was a white as a ghost. And a tear left his eye. "No," he stated. "Gracie and I are supposed to see the babies together, at the same time. I don't want to see them before her." Landon squeezed his shoulder.

"Mr. Conners, it could be days before Gracie wakes up. Now is a great time to bond with the babies."

"No. I won't see them before Gracie."

Annie stepped forward and put an arm around Jessie. "Can the babies go to the recovery room to be near Gracie?" she asked.

Dr. Shaw nodded. "Yes, after their baths and after they've been monitored for two hours, as is hospital policy, they can go to their mother's recovery room.

We usually don't allow babies in the ICU though. But I think we can make an exception. Would you like to accompany Mr. Conners' to his wife's room?" Dr. Shaw was grateful for Annie and her help.

"Yes, we would like to go Gracie's room. Jessie and I will wait there for the babies." Annie said.

She took Jessie by the arm and helped support him as he walked the halls of the hospital from the maternity ward down to the intensive care unit. Gracie had a needle in both arms, with numerous tubes coming out of them, all hooked up to bags and machines. He could see the bag that was giving her blood and wondered if he looked the same way after he was shot. The thought of Gracie seeing him like that made him weak at the knees. He pulled a chair next to the bed, grabbed Gracie's hand and wept like a baby.

Annie sat on the other side of her and silently cried as well. She was a grayish color, and her skin was cold. The ICU nurse came in, and Jessie tried to compose himself. "Is she in any pain?" he asked.

"No sir!" the nurse said quickly. "You see this tube here? This one is giving her pain medicine. Did Dr. Shaw tell you about her incision?" Jessie nodded. "Let me show it to you." She pulled down the blanket to just above Gracie's pelvic bone, and then pulled up her gown they had laid over her. "Usually for C-sections, the incision goes sideways. But since this was an emergency and they had to get the babies out quickly, her incision goes up and down." Jessie got queasy at the sight of her incision going from her naval to her pelvic bone. "This is going to take a little longer to heal, but once it does, she won't have any problems! The scar will fade over time too."

The nurse spent over thirty minutes explaining everything that was going on with Gracie. Every tub, every beep of the machine, every medication she was being given. Jessie somehow felt better after the nurse had explained everything. He at least felt like he knew what was happening to her.

The two hours the babies were in the nursery flew by. Jessie had his head on the bed next to Gracie's and was startled by a knock at the door. The maternity nurse was pushing a clear plastic bassinet with two little bundles in blankets – one in pink, one in blue.

The nurse smiled and pushed the bassinet over to Jessie. He was about to say no again because Gracie wasn't awake, but he couldn't take his eyes off his babies.

"Congratulations, Mr. Conners! You have a beautiful and healthy baby boy and girl. Your son was born at ten fifty-two pm. He weighs six pounds and seven ounces, eighteen inches, which is huge for a twin, and to be born early! No wonder your wife had complications! Your daughter was born at ten fifty-five pm. She weighs five pounds ten ounces, is sixteen inches long. She's a tiny little thing like your wife! They're both doing great!"

The nurse picked up the little blue bundle and placed him in Jessie's arm. Then she picked up the pink one, and put her in Jessie's other arm. He had never held a baby before, and now he was holding two of his own. They were both sleeping silently. The nurse went over their bottles and diapers, and then left the room.

Annie got up and walked over to Jessie to get a closer look at the babies. They were beautiful. "I have an idea!" she said, looking over her shoulder to make sure the ICU nurses weren't watching.

Annie took each baby, and laid them in Gracie's arms. She knew that nothing would keep Gracie from her babies and if she had any fight in her at all, the babies would bring it out. "Talk to her, Jessie. Tell her about the babies."

As Jessie started to relay the news about each baby, Gracie started to stir. Annie was right. Jessie looked over his shoulder at Annie and she smiled, then silently backed out of the room to give the new family their privacy.

It took a few minutes, but Gracie opened her eyes. She blinked a few times, then focused on Jessie.

Her throat hurt from the tube they stuck down it in surgery, but she had to know. "The babies," she whispered.

"They're in your arms," he said, touching a hand to her cheek. She looked down and saw them. All she could do was smile. "They're perfect. Big for twins. That's why there were complications. But they're fine," he told her.

"Hold them so I can see them." Her voice was wispy. Jessie took the cup of ice chips and placed one in her mouth. It felt good on her sore throat.

He held each baby up, one at a time. And like he wanted, they got to see their babies together, for the first time. He held up their son first, then their daughter. Finally the nurse came in and saw Gracie awake and talking.

"Congratulations, Mrs. Conners! How are you feeling?" the nurse asked.

"Happy," Gracie said.

"Once you're done with the babies, I'll take them back to the nursery. You can see them any time, but I think you need to get your rest. They can room with you when you're back on the maternity floor."

Gracie nodded and looked at Jessie. "Stay with them until they can stay with me," she said.

He shook his head. "Gracie, I need to stay with you."

She shook her head no, but didn't have the strength to argue.

He knew she was upset. "How about this? I'll make sure someone is with them at all times until they can stay in your room." She smiled and he gently kissed her lips.

* * *

Gracie spent three days in the ICU, and then was moved back to the surgical wing of the maternity floor. She was asking for the babies on the way up to her room. Nothing was going to keep her from them. She could finally have visitors and asked to see Timmy, Melissa, and Gavin immediately. Jessie had them on the way to the hospital before she was even settled.

Once inside her room, they brought the babies: Jessie Carson Conners II and Lilah Autumn Conners. She was holding both of them when she heard Timmy's loud voice coming down the hall.

She smiled at Jessie, as he ran into the room ahead of Melissa and Gavin. "You said you would never leave me!" Timmy yelled at her as he crawled into bed with her. She grimaced at the pain, and had Jessie help him gently lay next to her. She gave the babies to Melissa who was already crying before she entered the room.

"I did say that, didn't I?" Gracie answered.

"Why did you leave me again?" Timmy asked in a quiet voice.

Gracie was silent for a second. "Timmy, when I said I would never leave you again, I meant it. That doesn't mean there won't be times when I have to be gone for a few days."

"But you didn't tell me," he countered back.

"You were sleeping. Would you rather me wake you up to tell you next time?" she asked him, hiding a smile.

"Yes!" he said defiantly.

"Ok. Next time, I will wake you up to tell you. Now do you want to see your new little brother and sister?" She pointed to Melissa who was holding them.

Melissa sat down in the chair so Timmy could be at eye level with them.

"Their faces look scrunched up," Timmy exclaimed.

Everyone laughed. Jessie grabbed him and sat him on his lap. He missed the kid. "That's because they're babies. They won't always be like that."

He sat there looking at them, asking a thousand questions about babies. Melissa was in all her glory holding them. She was a nanny at heart. Children were her world. And Gracie didn't miss the wink Gavin gave her again.

* * *

Gracie stayed in the hospital for another week. Her asthma wouldn't settle down from the anesthesia, so they kept her a few extra days for prescription strength breathing treatments. The babies were doing great, gaining weight and taking their bottles like champs. Jessie lost count of the number of diapers he had changed.

When they finally got to go home, it was Gracie who was nervous instead of Jessie. "What if something goes wrong again?" she asked on the drive home. He was especially careful going over the bumps and taking the turns more slowly than usual.

"What could possibly go wrong?" Jessie asked. "You've already been kidnapped, had your death faked, killed a guy, gained custody of your brother, and almost died on me twice. I'd say you covered all the bases already."

"I'm serious! It's just going to be me and you and Timmy and the babies. Everyone said they were moving out, but I didn't believe them. I have three kids and two arms! How am I supposed to do this?"

"Annie moved into the room next to Timmy's. And I'm always going to be there."

She seemed satisfied with that. Jessie pulled the car up to the front door. He helped Gracie out while Annie and Melissa came outside to get the car seats. As they entered the house, Gracie's heart felt full. She had never had a feeling like this before. She had the man she loved, her baby brother, two beautiful babies, and a woman who was more like a mother to her than her own. Melissa had become her best friend, and the guys...they were her brothers. She truly had it all. She enjoyed the moment. Taking the babies out of their car seats, holding them in the living room while Brear and Honey sniffed them, listening to the pages of rules Timmy had made for them while she was still in the hospital.

That night, Gracie made Jessie move the bassinets into the bedroom. Across the loft was too far away to be from her newborns. Jessie swore he'd give Gracie anything she wanted if she'd just come back to him when she was lying helpless in the ICU. And he did. They sat on the edge of the bed marveling at Carson and Lilah.

"They're beautiful," Jessie said. "Just like their mama."

Gracie laid her head on his shoulder. "Thank you for abducting me."

They both laughed. Jessie kissed her, then both babies. They were going to be happy, and together.

"You know, they kept calling you my wife at the hospital," Jessie said as he pulled a small black box out of his pocket. "So I thought it was time to officially make you Mrs. Jessie Conners."

Gracie stared at the little black velvet box. "Jessie, you already asked me," Gracie said in disbelief. "I told you I don't need a ring."

"Open the box Gracie. You deserve your fairy tale ending."

Taking the box from Jessie, she slowly opened it. Gracie gasped at the three diamonds, surrounded by a band of diamond chips. There were so many diamonds on it, the ring sparkled in the dark.

"Marry me, Gracie," Jessie said.

Gracie was crying. "Do I have a choice?" she asked, reminiscent of older conversations they had in this very room.

Jessie smiled. "No. No you don't."

Gracie kissed him. "Of course I'll marry you!"

ANNIE LEE

* * *

Look for **Silently Love** early Summer 2011

* * *

Visit us online at AnnieLeeNovelist.com

annieleenovelist@yahoo.com

On Facebook at:

Annie Lee Fan Page

Keeping Grace Alive book page

At our website you'll find:

- ❖ Up-to-date author blogs
- ❖ Information about the author
- ❖ Current events
- ❖ Links
- ❖ Book release information
- ❖ New novel synopsis
- ❖ Early chapter releases
- ❖ Plus, much more!